A TOUCH OF DEAD

A Touch of Dead

SOOKIE STACKHOUSE:
THE COMPLETE STORIES

Charlaine Harris

WHEELER
CHIVERS

This Large Print edition is published by Wheeler Publishing, Waterville, Maine, USA and by BBC Audiobooks Ltd, Bath, England.
Wheeler Publishing, a part of Gale, Cengage Learning.
Collection copyright © 2009 by Charlaine Harris, Inc.
"Fairy Dust" copyright © 2004 by Charlaine Harris.
"Dracula Night" copyright © 2007 by Charlaine Harris.
"One Word Answer" copyright © 2005 by Charlaine Harris.
"Lucky" copyright © 2008 by Charlaine Harris, Inc.
"Gift Wrap" copyright © 2008 by Charlaine Harris, Inc.
The moral right of the author has been asserted.
Interior Art by Lisa Desimini.

The text of this Large Print edition is unabridged.
Other aspects of the book may vary from the original edition.
Set in 16 pt. Plantin.
Printed on permanent paper.

LIBRARY OF CONGRESS CATALOGING-IN-PUBLICATION DATA

Harris, Charlaine.
  A touch of dead : Sookie Stackhouse : the complete stories / by Charlaine Harris.
    p. cm.
  ISBN-13: 978-1-4104-2334-4 (alk. paper)
  ISBN-10: 1-4104-2334-4 (alk. paper)
  1. Vampires—Fiction. 2. Occult fiction, American. 3. Large type books. I. Title.
PS3558.A6427T68 2010
813'.54—dc22   2009045817

BRITISH LIBRARY CATALOGUING-IN-PUBLICATION DATA AVAILABLE

Published in 2010 in the U.S. by arrangement with The Berkley Publishing Group, a member of Penguin Group (USA) Inc.
Published in 2010 in the U.K. by arrangement with The Orion Publishing Group Ltd.

U.K. Hardcover: 978 1 408 47842 4 (Chivers Large Print)
U.K. Softcover: 978 1 408 47843 1 (Camden Large Print)

Printed in the United States of America
1 2 3 4 5 6 7 14 13 12 11 10

*For all those readers who want
every last sip of Sookie*

CONTENTS

CONTENTS

INTRODUCTION

The first time I was asked to write a short story about my heroine Sookie Stackhouse, I wasn't sure I could do it. Sookie's life and history are so complex that I didn't know if I could create a coherent piece of short fiction that would do her justice.

I'm still not sure I have, but I've enjoyed trying. Some efforts have been more successful than others. It's been hard to fit the stories into Sookie's larger history without leaving seams. Sometimes I succeeded, sometimes not. In this edition, I've tried to smooth out the edges of the story that was the most fun to write but wouldn't fit in its chronological hole no matter how I pounded ("Dracula Night").

In the order in which they occur in Sookie's life, the stories are "Fairy Dust" (from *Powers of Detection*), "Dracula Night" (from *Many Bloody Returns*), "One Word Answer" (from *Bite*), "Lucky" (from *Unusual Suspects*), and "Gift Wrap" (from *Wolfsbane and Mistletoe*).

"Fairy Dust" is about the fairy triplets Claude, Claudine, and Claudette. Following the murder of Claudette, Claude and Claudine seek Sookie's help in determining the guilty party. Claude acquires a valuable asset in this story. The action in "Fairy Dust" takes place after the events in *Dead to the World*.

In "Dracula Night," Eric invites Sookie to Fangtasia for the celebration of Dracula's birthday, an annual event that makes Eric almost over-the-top with anticipation, since Dracula is his hero. Unfortunately, the "Dracula" who unveils himself may or may not be the real thing. Eric celebrates "Dracula Night" before the action of *Dead as a Doornail.*

After *Dead as a Doornail,* the news of her cousin Hadley's death reaches Sookie in "One Word Answer." Sookie is informed of Hadley's demise by the half-demon lawyer Mr. Cataliades, who has a loathsome driver and an unexpected passenger in his limo.

"Lucky" is a lighthearted story set in Bon Temps in the time period after *All Together Dead.* Witch Amelia

Broadway and Sookie are on the hunt to find out who's sabotaging the town's insurance agents.

On Christmas Eve, Sookie receives a very unexpected visitor in "Gift Wrap." She's alone and feeling a little sorry for herself when a wounded werewolf supplies her with a satisfying gift. I'm pleased she has such an interesting holiday before the grim events of *Dead and Gone.*

I had a good time writing all these stories. Some are totally lighthearted, and some are more serious, but they all shine a light on a little facet of Sookie's life and times that I haven't recorded in the books. I hope you enjoy reading them as much as I enjoyed writing them.

Let the good times roll.

CHARLAINE HARRIS

■ ■ ■ ■

FAIRY DUST

■ ■ ■ ■

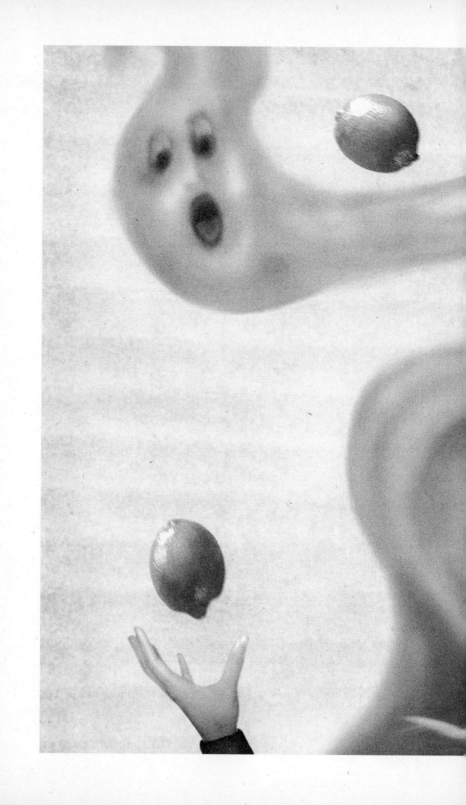

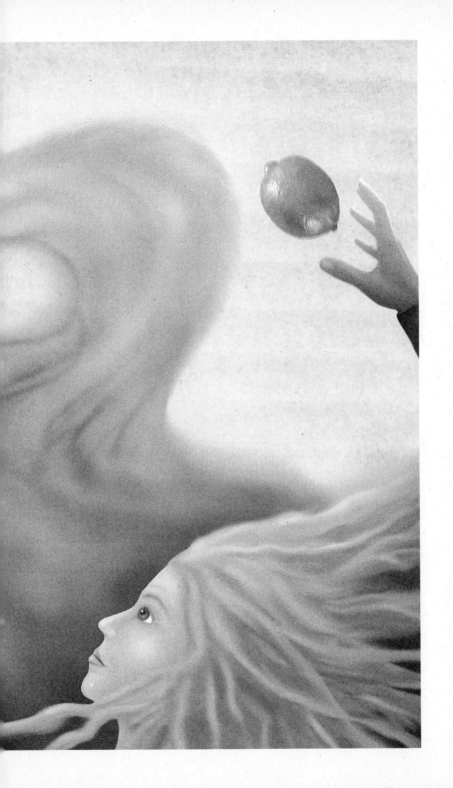

I hate it when fairies come into the bar. They don't tip you worth a toot — not because they're stingy, but because they just forget. Take Claudine, the fairy who was walking in the door. Six feet tall, long black hair, gorgeous; Claudine seemed to have no shortage of cash or clothing (and she entranced men the way a watermelon draws flies). But Claudine hardly ever remembered to leave you even a dollar. And if it's lunchtime, you have to take the bowl of lemon slices off the table. Fairies are allergic to lemons and limes, like vamps are allergic to silver and garlic.

That spring night when Claudine came in I was in a bad mood already. I was angry with my ex-boyfriend, Bill Compton, a.k.a. Vampire Bill; my brother, Jason, had again postponed helping me shift an armoire; and I'd gotten my property tax notice in the mail.

So when Claudine sat at one of my tables, I stalked over to her with no very happy feelings.

"No vamps around?" she asked straightaway. "Even Bill?"

Vamps like fairies the way dogs like bones: great toys, good food. "Not tonight," I said. "Bill's down in New Orleans. I'm picking up his mail for him." Just call me sucker.

Claudine relaxed. "Dearest Sookie,"

she said.

"You want what?"

"Oh, one of those nasty beers, I guess," she said, making a face. Claudine didn't really like to drink, though she did like bars. Like most fairies, she loved attention and admiration: my boss, Sam, said that was a fairy characteristic.

I brought her the beer. "You got a minute?" she asked. I frowned. Claudine didn't look as cheerful as usual.

"Just." The table by the door was hooting and hollering at me.

"I have a job for you."

Though it called for dealing with Claudine, whom I liked but didn't trust, I was interested. I sure needed some cash. "What do you need me to do?"

"I need you to come listen to some

humans."

"Are these humans willing?"

Claudine gave me innocent eyes. "What do you mean, Precious?"

I hated this song and dance. "Do they want to be, ah, listened to?"

"They're guests of my brother, Claude."

I hadn't known Claudine had a brother. I don't know much about fairies; Claudine was the only one I'd met. If she was typical, I wasn't sure how the race had survived eradication. I wouldn't have thought northern Louisiana was very hospitable toward beings of the fairy persuasion, anyway. This part of the state is largely rural, very Bible Belt. My small town of Bon Temps, barely big enough to have its own Wal-Mart, didn't even see a vampire for two years after they'd announced their existence and their intention to live peaceably amongst us. Maybe that delay was good, since local folks had had a chance to get used to the idea by the time Bill showed up.

But I had a feeling that this PC vamp tolerance would vanish if my fellow townsfolk knew about Weres, and shifters, and fairies. And who knows what all else.

"Okay, Claudine. When?"

The rowdy table was hooting, "Crazy Sookie! Crazy Sookie!" People only did that when they'd had too much to drink. I was used to it, but it still hurt.

"When do you get off tonight?"

We fixed it that Claudine would pick me up at my house fifteen minutes after I got off work. She left without finishing her beer. Or tipping.

My boss, Sam Merlotte, nodded a head toward the door through which she'd just exited. "What'd the fairy want?" Sam's a shifter himself.

"She needs me to do a job for her."

"Where?"

"Wherever she lives, I guess. She has a brother, did you know?"

"Want me to come with you?" Sam is a friend, the kind of friend you sometimes have fantasies about.

X-rated.

"Thanks, but I think I can handle Claudine."

"You haven't met the brother."

"I'll be okay."

I'm used to being up at night, not only because I'm a barmaid, but also because I had dated Bill for a long time. When Claudine picked me up at my old house in the woods, I'd had time to change from my Merlotte's outfit into some black jeans and a sage green twinset (JCPenney on sale), since the night was chilly. I'd let my hair down from its ponytail.

"You should wear blue instead of green," Claudine said, "to go with your eyes."

"Thanks for the fashion tip."

"You're welcome." Claudine sounded happy to share her style sense with me. But her smile, usually so radiant, seemed tinged with sadness.

"What do you want me to find out from these people?" I asked.

"We'll talk about it when we get there," she said, and after that she wouldn't tell me anything else as we drove east. Ordinarily Claudine babbles. I was beginning to feel it wasn't smart of me to have accepted this job.

Claudine and her brother lived in a big ranch-style house in suburban Monroe, a town that not only had a Wal-Mart, but a whole mall. She knocked on the front door in a pattern. After a minute, the door opened. My eyes widened. Claudine hadn't mentioned that her brother was her twin.

If Claude had put on his sister's clothes, he could have passed for her; it was eerie. His hair was shorter, but not by a lot; he had it pulled back to the nape of his neck, but his ears were covered. His shoulders were broader, but I couldn't see a trace of a beard, even this late at night. Maybe male fairies don't have body hair? Claude looked like a Calvin Klein underwear model; in fact, if the designer had been there, he'd have signed the twins on the spot, and there'd have been drool all over the contract.

Claude stepped back to let us enter. "This is the one?" he said to Claudine.

She nodded. "Sookie, my brother, Claude."

"A pleasure," I said. I extended my hand. With some surprise, he took it and shook. He looked at his sister. "She's a trusting one."

"Humans," Claudine said, and shrugged.

Claude led me through a very conventional living room, down a paneled hall to the family room. A man was sitting in a chair, because he had no choice. He was tied to it with what looked like nylon cord. He was a small man, buff, blond, and brown-eyed. He looked about my age, twenty-six.

"Hey," I said, not liking the squeak in my voice, "why is that man tied?"

"Otherwise, he'd run away," Claude said, surprised.

I covered my face with my hands for a second. "Listen, you two, I don't mind looking at this guy if he's done something wrong, or if you want to eliminate him as a suspect in a crime committed against you. But if you just want to find out if he really loves you, or something silly like that . . . What's your purpose?"

"We think he killed our triplet, Claudette."

I almost said, "There were three of you?" then realized that wasn't the most important part of the sentence.

"You think he murdered your sister."

Claudine and Claude nodded in unison. "Tonight," Claude said.

"Okeydokey," I muttered, and bent over the blond. "I'm taking the gag off."

They looked unhappy, but I slid the handkerchief down to his neck. The young man said, "I didn't do it."

"Good. Do you know what I am?"

"No. You're not a thing like them, are you?"

I don't know what he thought Claude and Claudine were, what little otherworldly attribute they'd sprung on him. I lifted my hair to show him that my ears were round, not pointed, but he still looked dissatisfied.

"Not a vamp?" he asked.

Showed him my teeth. The canines only extend when vamps are excited by blood, battle, or sex, but they're noticeably sharp even when they're retracted. My canines are quite normal.

"I'm just a regular human," I said. "Well, that's not quite true. I can read your thoughts."

He looked terrified.

"What are you scared for? If you didn't kill anybody, you have nothing to fear." I made my voice warm, like butter melting on corn on the cob.

"What will they do to me? What if you make a mistake and tell them I did it? What are they gonna do?"

Good question. I looked up at the two.

"We'll kill him and eat him," Claudine said, with a ravishing smile. When the blond man looked from her to Claude, his eyes wide with terror, she winked at me.

For all I knew, Claudine might be serious. I couldn't remember if I'd ever seen her eat or not. We were treading on dangerous ground. I try to support my own race when I can. Or at least get 'em out of situations alive.

I should have accepted Sam's offer.

"Is this man the only suspect?" I asked the twins. (Should I call them twins? I wondered. It was more accurate to think of them as two-thirds of triplets. Nah. Too complicated.)

"No, we have another man in the

kitchen," Claude said.

"And a woman in the pantry."

Under other circumstances, I would've smiled. "Why are you sure Claudette is dead?"

"She came to us in spirit form and told us so." Claude looked surprised. "This is a death ritual for our race."

I sat back on my heels, trying to think of intelligent questions. "When this happens, does the spirit let you know any of the circumstances of the death?"

"No," Claudine said, shaking her head so her long black hair switched. "It's more like a final farewell."

"Have you found the body?"

They looked disgusted. "We fade," Claude explained, in a haughty way.

So much for examining the corpse.

"Can you tell me where Claudette

was when she, ah, faded?" I asked. "The more I know, the better questions I can ask." Mind reading is not so simple. Asking the right questions is the key to eliciting the correct thought. The mouth can say anything. The head never lies. But if you don't ask the right question, the right thought won't pop up.

"Claudette and Claude are exotic dancers at Hooligans," Claudine said proudly, as if she was announcing they were on an Olympic team.

I'd never met strippers before, male or female. I found myself more than a little interested in seeing Claude strip, but I made myself focus on the deceased Claudette.

"So, Claudette worked last night?"

"She was scheduled to take the money at the door. It was ladies' night at Hooligans."

"Oh. Okay. So you were, ah, performing," I said to Claude.

"Yes. We do two shows on ladies' night. I was the Pirate."

I tried to suppress that mental image.

"And this man?" I tilted my head toward the blond, who was being very good about not pleading and begging.

"I'm a stripper, too," he said. "I was the Cop."

Okay. Just stuff that imagination in a box and sit on it.

"Your name is?"

"Barry Barber is my stage name. My real name is Ben Simpson."

"Barry Barber?" I was puzzled.

"I like to shave people."

I had a blank moment, then felt a

red flush creep across my cheeks as I realized he didn't mean whiskery cheeks. Well, not facial cheeks. "And the other two people are?" I asked the twins.

"The woman in the pantry is Rita Child. She owns Hooligans," Claudine said. "And the man in the kitchen is Jeff Puckett. He's the bouncer."

"Why did you pick these three out of all the employees at Hooligans?"

"Because they had arguments with Claudette. She was a dynamic woman," Claude said seriously.

"Dynamic my ass," said Barry the Barber, proving that tact isn't a prerequisite for a stripping job. "That woman was hell on wheels."

"Her character isn't really important in determining who killed her," I

33

pointed out, which shut him right up. "It just indicates why. Please go on," I said to Claude. "Where were the three of you? And where were the people you've held here?"

"Claudine was here, cooking supper for us. She works at Dillard's in customer service." She'd be great at that; her unrelenting cheer could pacify anyone. "As I said, Claudette was scheduled to take the cover charge at the door," Claude continued. "Barry and I were in both shows. Rita always puts the first show's take in the safe, so Claudette won't be sitting up there with a lot of cash. We've been robbed a couple of times. Jeff was mostly sitting behind Claudette, in a little booth right inside the main door."

"When did Claudette vanish?"

"Soon after the second show started. Rita says she got the first show's take from Claudette and took it back to her safe, and that Claudette was still sitting there when she left. But Rita hates Claudette, because Claudette was about to leave Hooligans for Foxes, and I was going with her."

"Foxes is another club?" Claude nodded. "Why were you leaving?"

"Better pay, larger dressing rooms."

"Okay, that would be Rita's motivation. What about Jeff's?"

"Jeff and I had a thing," Claude said. (My pirate-ship fantasy sank.) "Claudette told me I had to break up with him, that I could do better."

"And you listened to her advice about your love life?"

"She was the oldest, by several

minutes," he said simply. "But I lo—
I am very fond of him."

"What about you, Barry?"

"She ruined my act," Barry said sullenly.

"How'd she do that?"

"She yelled, 'Too bad your nightstick's not bigger!' as I was finishing up."

It seemed that Claudette had been determined to die.

"Okay," I said, marshaling my plan of action. I knelt before Barry. I laid my hand on his arm, and he twitched. "How old are you?"

"Twenty-five," he said, but his mind provided me with a different answer.

"That's not right, is it?" I asked, keeping my voice gentle.

He had a gorgeous tan, almost as good as mine, but he paled underneath it. "No," he said in a strangled voice. "I'm thirty."

"I had no idea," Claude said, and Claudine told him to hush.

"And why didn't you like Claudette?"

"She insulted me in front of an audience," he said. "I told you."

The image from his mind was quite different. "In private? Did she say something to you in private?" After all, reading minds isn't like watching television. People don't relate things in their own brains the way they would if they were telling a story to another person.

Barry looked embarrassed and even angrier. "Yes, in private. We'd been having sex for a while, and then one day she just wasn't interested anymore."

"Did she tell you why?"

"She told me I was . . . inadequate."

That hadn't been the phrase she used. I felt embarrassed for him when I heard the actual words in his head.

"What did you do between shows tonight, Barry?"

"We had an hour. So I could get two shaves in."

"You get paid for that?"

"Oh, yeah." He grinned, but not as though something was funny. "You think I'd shave a stranger's crotch if I didn't get paid for it? But I make a big ritual out of it; act like it turns me on. I get a hundred bucks a pop."

"When did you see Claudette?"

"When I went out to meet my first appointment, right as the first show was ending. She and her boyfriend were standing by the booth. I'd told them that was where I'd meet them."

"Did you talk to Claudette?"

"No, I just looked at her." He sounded sad. "I saw Rita, she was on her way to the booth with the money pouch, and I saw Jeff, he was on the stool at the back of the booth, where he usually stays."

"And then you went back to do this shaving?"

He nodded.

"How long does it take you?"

"Usually about thirty, forty minutes. So scheduling two was kind of chancy, but it worked out. I do it in the dressing room, and the other guys are good about staying out."

He was getting more relaxed, the thoughts in his head calming and flowing more easily. The first person he'd done tonight had been a woman so bone-thin he'd wondered if she'd die while he did the shaving routine. She'd thought she was beautiful, and she'd obviously enjoyed showing him her body. Her boyfriend had gotten a kick out of the whole thing.

I could hear Claudine buzzing in the background, but I kept my eyes closed and my hands on Barry's, seeing the second "client," a guy, and then I saw his face. Oh, boy. It was someone I knew, a vampire named Maxwell Lee.

"There was a vamp in the bar," I said, out loud, not opening my eyes. "Barry, what did he do when you finished shaving him?"

"He left," Barry said. "I watched him go out the back door. I'm always careful to make sure my clients are out of the backstage area. That's the

40

only way Rita will let me do the shaving at the club."

Of course, Barry didn't know about the problem fairies have with vamps. Some vamps had less self-control when it came to fairies than others did. Fairies were strong, stronger than people, but vamps were stronger than anything else on earth.

"And you didn't go back out to the booth and talk to Claudette again?"

"I didn't see her again."

"He's telling the truth," I said to Claudine and Claude. "As far as he knows it." There were always other questions I could ask, but at first "hearing," Barry didn't know anything about Claudette's disappearance.

Claude ushered me into the pantry, where Rita Child was waiting. It was a walk-in pantry, very neat, but not intended for two people, one of them duct-taped to a rolling office chair. Rita Child was a substantial woman, too. She looked exactly like I'd expect the owner of a strip club to look — painted, dyed brunette, packed into a challenging dress with high-tech underwear that pinched and pushed her into a provocative shape.

She was also steaming mad. She kicked out at me with a high heel that would have taken my eye out if I hadn't jerked back in the middle of kneeling in front of her. I fell on my fundament in an ungraceful sprawl.

"None of that, Rita," Claude said calmly. "You're not the boss here. This is our place." He helped me stand up and dusted off my bottom in an impersonal way.

"We just want to know what happened to our sister," Claudine said.

Rita made sounds behind her gag, sounds that didn't seem to be conciliatory. I got the impression that she didn't give a damn about the twins' motivation in kidnapping her and tying her up in their pantry. They'd taped her mouth, rather than using a cloth gag, and after the kicking incident, I kind of enjoyed ripping the tape off.

Rita called me some names reflecting on my heritage and moral character.

"I guess that's just the pot calling the kettle black," I said, when she paused to breathe. "Now you listen here! I'm not taking that kind of talk off of you, and I want you to shut up and answer my questions. You don't seem to have a good picture of the situation you're in."

The club owner calmed down a little bit after that. She was still glaring at me with her narrow brown eyes and straining at her ropes, but she seemed to understand a little better.

"I'm going to touch you," I said. I was afraid she might bite if I touched her bare shoulder, so I put my hand on her forearm just above where her wrists were tied to the arms of the rolling chair.

Her head was a maze of fury. She wasn't thinking clearly because she was so angry, and all her mental energy was directed into cursing at the twins and now at me. She suspected me of being some kind of supernatural assassin, and I decided it wouldn't hurt if she was scared of me for a while.

"When did you see Claudette to-night?" I asked.

"When I went to get the money from the first show," she growled, and sure enough, I saw Rita's hand reaching out, a long white hand placing a zippered vinyl pouch in it. "I was in my office working during the first show. But I get the money in between, so if we get stuck up, we won't lose so much."

"She gave you the money bag, and you left?"

"Yeah. I went to put the cash in the safe until the second show was over. I didn't see her again."

And that seemed to be the truth to me. I couldn't see another vision of Claudette in Rita's head. But I saw a lot of satisfaction that Claudette was dead, and a grim determination to keep Claude at her club.

"Will you still go to Foxes, now that Claudette's gone?" I asked him, to spark a response that might reveal something from Rita.

Claude looked down at me, surprised and disgusted. "I haven't had time to think of what will come tomorrow," he snapped. "I just lost my sister."

Rita's mind sort of leaped with joy. She had it bad for Claude. And on the practical side, he was a big draw at Hooligans, since even on an off night he could engender some magic to make the crowd spend big. Claudette hadn't been so willing to use her power for Rita's profit, but Claude didn't think about it twice. Using his inbred fairy skills to draw people to admire him was an ego thing with Claude, which had little to do with economics.

I got all this from Rita in a flash.

"Okay," I said, standing up. "I'm through with her."

She was happy.

We stepped out of the pantry into the kitchen, where the final candidate for murderer was waiting. He'd been pushed under the table, and he had a glass in front of him with a straw stuck in it, so he could lean over to drink. Being a former lover had paid off for Jeff Puckett. His mouth wasn't even taped.

I looked from Claude to Jeff, trying to figure it out. Jeff had a light brown mustache that needed trimming, and a two-day growth of whiskers on his cheeks. His eyes were narrow and hazel. As much as I could tell, Jeff seemed to be in better shape than some of the bouncers I'd known, and he was even taller than Claude. But I was not impressed, and I reflected for maybe the millionth time that love was strange.

Claude braced himself visibly when he faced his former lover.

"I'm here to find out what you know about Claudette's death," I said, since we'd been around a corner when we'd questioned Rita. "I'm a telepath, and I'm going to touch you while I ask you some questions."

Jeff nodded. He was very tense. He fixed his eyes on Claude. I stood behind him, since he was pushed up under the table, and put my hands on his thick shoulders. I pulled his T-shirt to one side, just a little, so my thumb could touch his neck.

"Jeff, you tell me what you saw tonight," I said.

"Claudette came to take the money for the first set," he said. His voice was higher than I'd expected, and he was not from these parts. Florida, I thought. "I couldn't stand her because she messed with my personal life, and I didn't want to be with her. But that's what Rita told me to do, so I did. I sat on the stool and watched her take the money and put it into the money bag. She kept some in a money drawer to make change."

"Did she have trouble with any of the customers?"

"No. It was ladies' night, and the women don't give any trouble coming in. They did during the second set. I had to go haul a gal offstage who got a little too enthusiastic about our Construction Worker, but mostly I just sat on the stool and watched."

"When did Claudette vanish?"

"When I came back from getting that gal back to her table, Claudette was gone. I looked around for her, went and asked Rita if Claudette had said anything to her about having to take a break. I even checked the ladies' room. Wasn't till I went back in the booth that I seen the glittery stuff."

"What glittery stuff?"

"What we leave when we fade," Claude murmured. "Fairy dust."

Did they sweep it up and keep it? It would probably be tacky to ask.

"And next thing I knew, the second set was over and the club was closing, and I was checking backstage and everywhere for traces of Claudette, then I was here with Claude and Claudine."

He didn't seem too angry.

"Do you know anything about Claudette's death?"

"No. I wish I did. I know this is hard on Claude." His eyes were as fixed on Claude as Claude's were on him. "She separated us, but she's not in the picture anymore."

"I have to know," Claude said, through clenched teeth.

For the first time, I wondered what the twins would do if I couldn't discover the culprit. And that scary thought spurred my brain to greater activity.

"Claudine," I called. Claudine came in, with an apple in her hand. She was hungry, and she looked tired. I wasn't surprised. Presumably, she'd worked all day, and here she was, staying up all night, and grieving, to boot.

"Can you wheel Rita in here?" I asked. "Claude, can you go get Barry?"

When everyone was assembled in the kitchen, I said, "Everything I've seen and heard seems to indicate that Claudette vanished during the second show." After a second's consideration, they all nodded. Barry's and Rita's mouths had been gagged again, and I thought that was a good thing.

"During the first show," I said, going slow to be sure I got it right, "Claudette took up the money. Claude was onstage. Barry was onstage. Even when he wasn't onstage, he didn't come up to the booth. Rita was in her office."

There were nods all around.

"During the interval between shows, the club cleared out."

"Yeah," Jeff said. "Barry came up to meet his clients, and I checked to make sure everyone else was gone."

"So you were away from the booth a little."

"Oh, well, yeah, I guess. I do it so often, I didn't even think of that."

"And also during the interval, Rita came up to get the money pouch from Claudette."

Rita nodded emphatically.

"So, at the end of the interval, Barry's clients have left." Barry nodded. "Claude, what about you?"

"I went out to get some food during the interval," he said. "I can't eat a lot before I dance, but I had to eat something. I got back, and Barry was by himself and getting ready for the second show. I got ready, too."

"And I got back on the stool," Jeff said. "Claudette was back at the cash window. She was all ready, with the cash drawer and the stamp and the pouch. She still wasn't speaking to me."

"But you're sure it was Claudette?" I asked, out of the blue.

"Wasn't Claudine, if that's what you mean," he said. "Claudine's as sweet as Claudette was sour, and they even sit different."

Claudine looked pleased and threw her apple core in the garbage can. She smiled at me, already forgiving me for asking questions about her.

The apple.

Claude, looking impatient, began to

speak. I held up my hand. He stopped.

"I'm going to ask Claudine to take your gags off," I said to Rita and Barry. "But I don't want you to talk unless I ask you a question, okay?" They both nodded.

Claudine took the gags off, while Claude glared at me.

Thoughts were pounding through my head like a mental stampede.

"What did Rita do with the money pouch?"

"After the first show?" Jeff seemed puzzled. "Uh, I told you. She took it with her."

Alarm bells were going off mentally. Now I knew I was on the right track.

"You said that when you saw Claudette waiting to take the money for the second show, she had everything ready."

"Yeah. So? She had the hand stamp, she had the money drawer, and she had the pouch," Jeff said.

"Right. She had to have a second pouch for the second show. Rita had taken the first pouch. So when Rita came to get the first show's take, she had the second pouch in her hand, right?"

Jeff tried to remember. "Uh, I guess so."

"What about it, Rita?" I asked. "Did you bring the second pouch?"

"No," she said. "There were two in the booth at the beginning of the evening. I just took the one she'd used, then she had an empty one there for the take from the second show."

"Barry, did you see Rita walking to

the booth?"

The blond stripper thought frantically. I could feel every idea beating at the inside of my head.

"She had something in her hand," he said finally. "I'm sure of it."

"No," Rita shrieked. "It was there already!"

"What's so important about the pouch, anyway?" Jeff asked. "It's just a vinyl pouch with a zipper like banks give you. How could that hurt Claudette?"

"What if the inside were rubbed with lemon juice?"

Both the fairies flinched, horror on their faces.

"Would that kill Claudette?" I asked them.

Claude said, "Oh, yes. She was especially susceptible. Even lemon scent made her vomit. She had a terrible time on washday until we found out the fabric sheets were lemon scented. Claudine has to go to the store since so many things are scented with the foul smell."

Rita began screaming, a high-pitched car alarm shriek that just seemed to go on and on. "I swear I didn't do it!" she said. "I didn't! I didn't!" But her mind was saying, "Caught, caught, caught, caught."

"Yeah, you did it," I said.

The surviving brother and sister stood in front of the rolling chair. "Sign over the bar to us," Claude said.

"What?"

"Sign over the club to us. We'll even pay you a dollar for it."

"Why would I do that? You got no

body! You can't go to the cops! What are you gonna say? 'I'm a fairy. I'm allergic to lemons.' " She laughed. "Who's gonna believe that?"

Barry said weakly, "Fairies?"

Jeff didn't say anything. He hadn't known the triplets were allergic to lemons. He didn't realize his lover was a fairy. I worry about the human race.

"Barry should go," I suggested.

Claude seemed to rouse himself. He'd been looking at Rita the way a cat eyes a canary. "Good-bye, Barry," he said politely, as he untied the stripper. "I'll see you at the club tomorrow night. Our turn to take up the money."

"Uh, right," Barry said, getting to his feet.

Claudine's mouth had been moving

all the while, and Barry's face went blank and relaxed. "See you later, nice party," he said genially.

"Good to meet you, Barry," I said.

"Come see the show sometime." He waved at me and walked out of the house, Claudine shepherding him to the front door. She was back in a flash.

Claude had been freeing Jeff. He kissed him, said, "I'll call you soon," and gently pushed him toward the back door. Claudine did the same spell, and Jeff's face, too, relaxed utterly from its tense expression. " 'Bye," the bouncer called as he shut the door behind him.

"Are you gonna mojo me, too?" I asked, in a kind of squeaky voice.

"Here's your money," Claudine said. She took my hand. "Thank you,

Sookie. I think you can remember this, huh, Claude? She's been so good!" I felt like a puppy that'd remembered its potty-training lesson.

Claude considered me for a minute, then nodded. He turned his attention back to Rita, who'd been taking the time to climb out of her panic.

Claude produced a contract out of thin air. "Sign," he told Rita, and I handed him a pen that had been on the counter beneath the phone.

"You're taking the bar in return for your sister's life," she said, expressing her incredulity at what I considered a very bad moment.

"Sure."

She gave the two fairies a look of contempt. With a flash of her rings, she took up the pen and signed the contract. She pushed up to her feet, smoothed the skirt of her dress across her round hips, and tossed her head. "I'll be going now," she said. "I own another place in Baton Rouge. I'll just live there."

"You'll start running," Claude said.

"What?"

"You better run. You owe us money and a hunt for the death of our sister. We have the money, or at least the means to make it." He pointed at the contract. "Now we need the hunt."

"That's not fair."

Okay, that disgusted even me.

"Fair is only part of fairy as letters of the alphabet." Claudine looked formidable: not sweet, not dotty. "If you can dodge us for a year, you can live."

"A year!" Rita's situation seemed to be feeling more and more real to her by then. She was beginning to look desperate.

"Starting . . . now." Claude looked up from his watch. "Better go. We'll give ourselves a four-hour handicap."

"Just for fun," Claudine said.

"And, Rita?" Claude said, as Rita made for the door. She paused, looked back at him.

Claude smiled at her. "We won't use lemons."

■ ■ ■ ■

DRACULA
NIGHT

■ ■ ■ ■

I found the invitation in the mailbox at the end of my driveway. I had to lean out of my car window to open it, because I'd paused on my way to work after remembering I hadn't checked my mail in a couple of days. My mail was never interesting. I might get a flyer for Dollar General or Wal-Mart, or one of those ominous mass mailings about pre-need burial plots.

Today, after I'd sighed at my Entergy bill and my cable bill, I had a little treat: a handsome, heavy, buff-colored envelope that clearly contained some kind of invitation. It had been addressed by someone who'd not only taken a calligraphy class but passed the final with flying colors.

I got a little pocketknife out of my glove compartment and slit open the envelope with the care it deserved. I don't get a lot of invitations, and when I do, they're usually more Hallmark than watermark. This was something to be savored. I carefully pulled out the stiff, folded paper and opened it. Something fluttered into my lap: an enclosed sheet of tissue. Without absorbing the revealed words, I ran my finger over the embossing. Wow.

I'd strung out the preliminaries as long as I could. I bent to actually read the italic typeface.

Eric Northman
and the Staff of Fangtasia

Request the honor of your
presence
at Fangtasia's annual party
to celebrate the birthday of the
Lord of Darkness

Prince Dracula

On January 13, 10:00 p.m.
music provided by the Duke of
Death
Dress Formal   RSVP

I read it twice. Then I read it again.
I drove to work in such a thoughtful mood that I'm glad there wasn't
any other traffic on Hummingbird
Road. I took the left to get to Merlotte's, but then I almost sailed right

past the parking lot. At the last moment, I braked and turned in to navigate my way to the parking area behind the bar that was reserved for employees.

Sam Merlotte, my boss, was sitting behind his desk when I peeked in to put my purse in the deep drawer in his desk that he let the servers use. He had been running his hands over his hair again, because the tangled red gold halo was even wilder than usual. He looked up from his tax form and smiled at me.

"Sookie," he said, "how are you doing?"

"Good. Tax season, huh?" I made sure my white T-shirt was tucked in evenly so that the MERLOTTE'S embroidered over my left breast would be level. I flicked one of my long blond hairs off my black pants. I always bent over to brush my hair out so my ponytail would look smooth. "You not taking them to the CPA this year?"

"I figure if I start this early, I can do them myself."

He said that every year, and he always ended up making an appointment with the CPA, who always had to file for an extension.

"Listen, did you get one of these?" I asked, extending the invitation.

He dropped his pen with some relief and took the sheet from my hand. After scanning the script, he said, "No. They wouldn't invite many shifters, anyway. Maybe the local packmaster, or some supe who'd done them a significant service . . . like you."

"I'm not supernatural," I said, surprised. "I just have a . . . problem."

"Telepathy is a lot more than a problem," Sam said. "Acne is a problem. Shyness is a problem. Reading other people's minds is a gift."

"Or a curse," I said. I went around the desk to toss my purse in the drawer, and Sam stood up. I'm around five foot six, and Sam tops me by maybe three inches. He's not a big guy, but he's much stronger than a plain human his size, since Sam's a shapeshifter.

"Are you going to go?" he asked. "Halloween and Dracula's birthday are the only holidays vampires observe, and I understand they can throw quite a party."

"I haven't made up my mind," I said. "When I'm on my break later, I might call Pam." Pam, Eric's second-in-command, was as close to a friend as I had among the vampires.

I reached her at Fangtasia pretty soon after the sun went down. "There really was a Count Dracula? I thought he was made up," I said after telling her I'd gotten the invitation.

"There really was," Pam said. "Vlad Tepes. He was a Wallachian king whose capital city was Târgovişte, I think." Pam was quite matter-of-fact about the existence of a creature I'd thought was a joint creation of Bram Stoker and Hollywood. "Vlad III was more ferocious and bloodthirsty than any vampire, and this was when he was a live human. He enjoyed executing people by impaling them on huge wooden stakes. They might last for hours."

I shuddered. Ick.

"His own people regarded him with fear, of course. But the local vamps admired Vlad so much they actually brought him over when he was dying, thus ushering in the new era of the vampire. After monks buried him on an island called Snagov, he rose on the third night to become the first modern vampire. Up until then, the vampires were like . . . well, disgusting. Completely secret. Ragged, filthy, living in holes in cemeteries, like animals. But Vlad Dracul had been a ruler, and he wasn't going to dress in rags and live in a hole for any reason." Pam sounded proud.

I tried to imagine Eric wearing rags and living in a hole, but it was almost impossible. "So Stoker didn't just dream the whole thing up based on folktales?"

"Just parts of it. Obviously, he didn't know a lot about what Dracula, as he called him, really could or couldn't do, but he was so excited at meeting the prince that he made up a lot of details he thought would give the story zing. It was just like Anne Rice meeting Louis: an early *Interview with the Vampire.* Dracula really wasn't too happy afterward that Stoker caught him at a weak moment, but he did enjoy the name recognition."

"But he won't actually be there, right? I mean, vampires'll be celebrating this all over the world."

Pam said, very cautiously, "Some believe he shows up somewhere every year, makes a surprise appearance. That chance is so remote, his appearance at our party would be like winning the lottery. Though some believe it could happen."

I heard Eric's voice in the background saying, "Pam, who are you talking to?"

"Okay," Pam said, the word sounding very American with her slight British accent. "Got to go, Sookie. See you then."

As I hung up the office phone, Sam said, "Sookie, if you go to the party, please keep alert and on the watch. Sometimes vamps get carried away with the excitement on Dracula Night."

"Thanks, Sam," I said. "I'll sure be careful." No matter how many vamps you claimed as friends, you had to be alert. A few years ago the Japanese had invented a synthetic blood that satisfies the vampires' nutritional requirements, which has enabled the undead to come out of the shadows and take their place at the American table. British vampires had it pretty good, too, and most of the Western European vamps had fared pretty well after the Great Revelation (the day they'd announced their existence, through carefully chosen representatives). However, many South American vamps regretted stepping forward, and the bloodsuckers in the Muslim countries — well, there were mighty few left. Vampires in the inhospitable parts of the world were making efforts to immigrate to countries that tolerated them, with the result that our Congress was considering various bills to limit undead citizens from claiming political asylum. In consequence, we were experiencing an influx of vampires with all kinds of accents as they tried to enter America under the wire. Most of them came in through Louisiana, since it was notably friendly to the Cold Ones, as *Fangbanger Xtreme* called them.

It was more fun thinking about vampires than hearing the thoughts of my fellow citizens. Naturally, as I went from table to table, I was doing my job with a big smile, because I like good tips, but I wasn't able to put my heart into it tonight. It had been a warm day for January, way into the fifties, and people's thoughts had turned to spring.

I try not to listen in, but I'm like a radio that picks up a lot of signals. Some days, I can control my reception a lot better than other days. Today, I kept picking up snippets. Hoyt Fortenberry, my brother's best friend, was thinking about his mom's plan for Hoyt to put in about ten new rosebushes in her already extensive garden. Gloomy but obedient, he was trying to figure out how much time the task would take. Arlene, my long-time friend and another waitress, was wondering if she could get her latest boyfriend to pop the question, but that was pretty much a perennial thought for Arlene. Like the roses, it bloomed every season.

As I mopped up spills and hustled to get chicken strip baskets on the tables (the supper crowd was heavy that night), my own thoughts were centered on how to get a formal gown to wear to the party. Though I did have one ancient prom dress, handmade by my aunt Linda, it was hopelessly outdated. I'm twenty-six, but I didn't have any bridesmaid dresses that might serve. None of my few friends had gotten married except Arlene, who'd been wed so many times that she never even thought of bridesmaids. The few nice clothes I'd bought for vampire events always seemed to get ruined . . . some in very unpleasant ways.

Usually, I shopped at my friend Tara's store, but she wasn't open after six. So after I got off work, I drove to Monroe to Pecanland Mall. At Dillard's, I got lucky. To tell the truth, I was so pleased with the dress I might have gotten it even if it hadn't been on sale, but it had been marked down to twenty-five dollars from a hundred and fifty, surely a shopping triumph. It was rose pink, with a sequin top and a chiffon bottom, and it was strapless and simple. I'd wear my hair down, and my gran's pearl earrings, and some silver heels that were also on major sale.

That important item taken care of, I wrote a polite acceptance note and popped it in the mail. I was good to go.

Three nights later, I was knocking on the back door of Fangtasia, my garment bag held high.

"You're looking a bit informal," Pam said as she let me in.

"Didn't want to wrinkle the dress." I came in, making sure the bag didn't trail, and hightailed it for the bath-room.

There wasn't a lock on the bathroom door. Pam stood outside so I wouldn't be interrupted, and Eric's second-in-command smiled when I came out, a bundle of my more mundane clothes rolled under my arm.

"You look good, Sookie," Pam said. Pam herself had elected to wear a tuxedo made out of silver lamé. She was a sight. My hair has some curl to it, but Pam's is a paler blond and very straight. We both have blue eyes, but hers are a lighter shade and rounder, and she doesn't blink much. "Eric will be very pleased."

I flushed. Eric and I have a History. But since he had amnesia when we created that history, he doesn't remember it. Pam does. "Like I care what he thinks," I said.

Pam smiled at me sideways. "Right," she said. "You are totally indifferent. So is he."

I tried to look like I was accepting her words on their surface level and not seeing through to the sarcasm. To my surprise, Pam gave me a light kiss on the cheek. "Thanks for coming," she said. "You may perk him up. He's been very hard to work for these past few days."

"Why?" I asked, though I wasn't real sure I wanted to know.

"Have you ever seen *It's the Great Pumpkin, Charlie Brown?*"

I stopped in my tracks. "Sure," I said. "Have *you?*"

"Oh, yes," Pam said calmly. "Many times." She gave me a minute to absorb that. "Eric is like that on Dracula Night. He thinks, every year, that this time Dracula will pick *his* party to attend. Eric fusses and plans;

he frets and stews. He sent the invitations back to the printer twice so they were late going out. Now that the night is actually here, he's worked himself into a state."

"So this is a case of hero worship gone crazy?"

"You have such a way with words," Pam said admiringly. We were outside Eric's office, and we could both hear him bellowing inside.

"He's not happy with the new bartender. He thinks there are not enough bottles of the blood the count is said to prefer, according to an interview in *American Vampire*."

I tried to imagine Vlad Tepes, impaler of so many of his own countrymen, chatting with a reporter. I sure wouldn't want to be the one holding the pad and pencil. "What brand would that be?" I scrambled to catch up with the conversation.

"The Prince of Darkness is said to prefer Royalty."

"Ew." Why was I not surprised?

Royalty was a very, very rare bottled blood. I'd thought the brand was only a rumor until now. Royalty consisted of part synthetic blood and part real blood — the blood of, you guessed it, people of title. Before you go thinking of enterprising vamps ambushing that cute Prince William, let me reassure you. There were plenty of minor royals in Europe who were glad to give blood for an astronomical sum.

"After a month's worth of phone calls, we managed to get two bottles." Pam was looking quite grim. "They cost more than we could afford. I've never known my maker to be other than business-wise, but this year Eric seems to be going overboard. Royalty doesn't keep forever, you know, with the real blood in it . . . and now he's worried that two bottles might not be enough. There is so much legend attached to Dracula, who can say what is true? He has heard that Dracula will only drink Royalty or . . . the real thing."

"Real blood? But that's illegal, unless you've got a willing donor."

Any vampire who took a human's blood — against the human's will — was liable to execution by stake or sunlight, according to the vamp's choice. The execution was usually carried out by another vamp, kept on retainer by the state. I personally thought any vampire who took an unwilling person's blood deserved the execution, because there were enough fangbangers around who were more than willing to donate.

"And no vampire is allowed to kill Dracula, or even strike him," Pam said, chiming right in on my thoughts. "Not that we'd want to strike our prince, of course," she added hastily.

Right, I thought.

"He is held in such reverence that any vampire who assaults him must meet the sun. And we're also expected to offer our prince financial assistance."

I wondered if the other vampires were supposed to floss his fangs for him, too.

The door to Eric's office flew open with such vehemence that it bounced right back. It opened again more gently, and Eric emerged.

I had to gape. He looked positively edible. Eric is very tall, very broad, very blond, and tonight he was dressed in a tuxedo that had not come off any rack. This tux had been made for Eric, and he looked as good as any James Bond in it. Black cloth without a speck of lint, a snowy white shirt, and a hand-tied bow at his throat, with his beautiful hair rippling down his back . . .

"James Blond," I muttered. Eric's eyes were blazing with excitement. Without a word, he dipped me as though we were dancing and planted a hell of a kiss on me: lips, tongue, the entire osculant assemblage. Oh boy, oh boy, oh boy. When I was quivering, he assisted me to rise. His brilliant smile revealed glistening fangs. Eric had enjoyed himself.

"Hello to you, too," I said tartly, once I was sure I was breathing again.

"My delicious friend," Eric said, and bowed.

I wasn't sure I could be correctly called a friend, and I'd have to take his word for it that I was delicious. "What's the program for the evening?" I asked, hoping that my host would calm down very soon.

"We'll dance, listen to music, drink blood, watch the entertainment, and wait for the count to come," Eric said. "I'm so glad you'll be here tonight. We have a wide array of special guests, but you're the only telepath."

"Okay," I said faintly.

"You look especially lovely tonight,"

said Lyle. He'd been standing right behind Eric, and I hadn't even noticed him. Slight and narrow-faced, with spiked black hair, Lyle didn't have the presence Eric had acquired in a thousand years of life. Lyle was a visiting vamp from Alexandria, interning at the very successful Fangtasia because he wanted to open his own vampire bar. Lyle was carrying a small cooler, taking great care to keep it level.

"The Royalty," Pam explained in a neutral voice.

"Can I see?" I asked.

Eric lifted the lid and showed me the contents: two blue bottles (for the blue blood, I presumed), with labels that bore the logo of a tiara and the single word "Royalty" in gothic script.

"Very nice," I said, underwhelmed.

"He'll be so pleased," Eric said, sounding as happy as I'd ever heard him.

"You sound oddly sure that the — that Dracula will be coming," I said. The hall was crowded, and we began moving to the public part of the club.

"I was able to have a business discussion with the Master's handler," he said. "I was able to express how much having the Master's presence would honor me and my establishment."

Pam rolled her eyes at me.

"You bribed him," I translated. Hence Eric's extra excitement this year, and his purchase of the Royalty.

I had never suspected Eric harbored this depth of hero worship for anyone except himself. I would never have believed he would spend good money for such a reason, either. Eric was charming and enterprising, and he took good care of his employees; but the first person on Eric's admiration list was Eric, and his own well-being was Eric's number one priority.

"Dear Sookie, you're looking less than excited," Pam said, grinning at me. Pam loved to make trouble, and she was finding fertile ground tonight. Eric swung his head back to give me a look, and Pam's face relaxed into its usual bland smoothness.

"Don't you believe it will happen, Sookie?" he asked. From behind his back, Lyle rolled his eyes. He was clearly fed up with Eric's fantasy.

I'd just wanted to come to a party in a pretty dress and have a good time, and here I was, up a conversational creek.

"We'll all find out, won't we?" I said brightly, and Eric seemed satisfied. "The club looks beautiful." Normally, Fangtasia was the plainest place you could imagine, besides the lively gray and red paint scheme and the neon. The floors were concrete, the tables and chairs basic metal restaurant furnishings, the booths not much better. I could not believe that Fangtasia had been so transformed. Banners had been hung from the club's ceiling. Each banner was white with a red bear on it: a sort of stylized bear on its hind legs, one paw raised to strike.

"That's a replica of the Master's personal flag," Pam said in answer to my pointed finger. "Eric paid an historian at LSU to research it." Her expression made it clear she thought Eric had been gypped, big-time.

In the center of Fangtasia's small dance floor stood an actual throne on a small dais. As I neared the throne, I decided Eric had rented it from a theater company. It looked good from thirty feet away, but up close . . . not so much. However, it had been freshened up with a plump red cushion for the Dark Prince's derriere, and the dais was placed in the exact middle of a square of dark red carpet. All the tables had been covered with white or dark red cloths, and elaborate flower arrangements were in the middle of each table. I had to laugh when I examined one of the arrangements: in the explosion of red carnations and greenery were miniature coffins and full-size stakes. Eric's sense of humor had surfaced, finally.

Instead of WDED, the all-vampire radio station, the sound system was playing some very emotional violin music that was both scratchy and bouncy. "Transylvanian music," said Lyle, his face carefully expression-less. "Later, the DJ Duke of Death will take us for a musical journey." Lyle looked as though he would rather eat snails.

Against one wall by the bar, I spied a small buffet for beings who ate food, and a large blood fountain for those who didn't. The red fountain, flowing gently down several tiers of gleaming milky glass bowls, was sur-rounded by crystal goblets. Just a wee bit over the top.

"Golly," I said weakly as Eric and Lyle went over to the bar.

Pam shook her head in despair. "The money we spent," she said.

Not too surprisingly, the room was full of vampires. I recognized a few of the bloodsuckers present: Indira, Thalia, Clancy, Maxwell Lee, and Bill Compton, my ex. There were at least twenty more I had only seen once or twice, vamps who lived in Area Five under Eric's authority. There were a few bloodsuckers I didn't know at all, including a guy behind the bar who must be the new bartender. Fangtasia ran through bartenders pretty quickly.

There were also some creatures in the bar who were not vamps and not human, members of Louisiana's supernatural community. The head of

Shreveport's werewolf pack, Colonel Flood, was sitting at a table with Calvin Norris, the leader of the small community of werepanthers who lived in and around Hot Shot, outside of Bon Temps. Colonel Flood, now retired from the air force, was sitting stiffly erect in a good suit, while Calvin was wearing his own idea of party clothes — a western shirt, new jeans, cowboy boots, and a black cowboy hat. He tipped it to me when he caught my eye, and he gave me a nod that expressed admiration. Colonel Flood's nod was less personal but still friendly.

Eric had also invited a short, broad man who strongly reminded me of a goblin I'd met once. I was sure this male was a member of the same race. Goblins are testy and ferociously strong, and when they are angry, their touch can burn, so I decided to stay a good distance away from this one. He was deep in conversation with a very thin woman with mad eyes. She was wearing an assemblage of leaves and vines. I wasn't going to ask.

Of course, there weren't any fairies. Fairies are as intoxicating to vampires as sugar water is to hummingbirds.

Behind the bar was the newest member of the Fangtasia staff, a short, burly man with long, wavy dark hair. He had a prominent nose and large eyes, and he was taking everything in with an air of amusement while he moved around preparing drink orders.

"Who's that?" I asked, nodding toward the bar. "And who are the strange vamps? Is Eric expanding?"

Pam said, "If you're in transit on Dracula Night, the protocol is to check in at the nearest sheriff's head-quarters and share in the celebration there. That's why there are vampires here you haven't met. The new bar-tender is Milos Griesniki, a recent immigrant from the Old Countries. He is disgusting."

I stared at Pam. "How so?" I asked.

"A sneaker. A pryer."

I'd never heard Pam express such a strong opinion, and I looked at the vampire with some curiosity.

"He tries to discover how much money Eric has, and how much the bar makes, and how much our little human barmaids get paid."

"Speaking of whom, where are they?" The waitresses and the rest of

the everyday staff, all vampire group-
ies (known in some circles as
fangbangers), were usually much in
evidence, dressed in filmy black and
powdered almost as pale as the real
vampires.

"Too dangerous for them on this
night," Pam said simply. "You will see
that Indira and Clancy are serving
the guests." Indira was wearing a
beautiful sari; she usually wore jeans
and T-shirts, so I knew she had made
an effort to dress up for the occasion.
Clancy, who had rough red hair and
bright green eyes, was in a suit. That
was also a first. Instead of a regular
tie, he wore a scarf tied into a floppy
bow, and when I caught his eye, he
swept his hand from his head to his
pants to demand my admiration. I
smiled and nodded, though truthfully

I liked Clancy better in his usual tough-guy clothes and heavy boots.

Eric was buzzing from table to table. He hugged and bowed and talked like a demented thing, and I didn't know if I found this endearing or alarming. I decided it was both. I'd definitely discovered Eric's weak side.

I talked to Colonel Flood and Calvin for a few minutes. Colonel Flood was as polite and distant as he always was; he didn't care much for non-Weres, and now that he had retired, he only dealt with regular people when he had to. Calvin told me that he'd put a new roof on his house himself, and invited me to go fishing with him when the weather was warmer. I smiled but didn't commit to anything. My grandmother had loved fishing, but I was only good for two hours, tops, and then I was ready to do something else. I watched Pam doing her second-in-command job, making sure all the visiting vampires were happy, sharply admonishing the new bartender when he made a mistake with a drink order. Milos Griesniki gave her back a scowl that made me shiver. But if anyone could take care of herself, it was Pam.

Clancy, who'd been managing the club for a month, was checking every table to make sure there were clean ashtrays (some of the vampires smoked) and that all dirty glasses and other discarded items were removed promptly. When DJ Duke of Death took over, the music changed to something with a beat. Some of the vampires turned out onto the dance floor, flinging themselves around with the extreme abandon only the un-dead show.

Calvin and I danced a couple of times, but we were nowhere in the vampire league. Eric claimed me for a slow dance, and though he was clearly distracted by thoughts of what the night might hold — Dracula-wise — he made my toenails quiver.

"Some night," he whispered, "there's going to be nothing else but you and me."

When the song was over, I had to go back to the table and have a long, cold drink. Lots of ice.

As the time drew closer to mid-night, the vampires gathered around the blood fountain and filled the crystal goblets. The non-vamp guests also rose to their feet. I was standing beside the table where I'd been chatting with Calvin and Colonel Flood when Eric brought out a tabletop hand gong and began to strike it. If he'd been human, he'd have been flushed with excitement; as it was, his eyes were blazing. Eric looked both beautiful and scary, because he was so intent.

When the last reverberation had shivered into silence, Eric raised his own glass high and said, "On this most memorable of days, we stand together in awe and hope that the Lord of Darkness will honor us with his presence. O Prince, appear to us!"

We actually all stood in hushed silence, waiting for the Great Pumpkin — oh, wait, the Dark Prince. Just when Eric's face began to look downcast, a harsh voice broke the tension.

"My loyal son, I shall reveal myself!"

Milos Griesniki leaped from behind the bar, pulling off his tux jacket and pants and shirt to reveal . . . an incredible jumpsuit made from black, glittery stretchy stuff. I would have expected to see it on a girl going to her prom, a girl without much money who was trying to look unconventional and sexy. With his blocky body and dark hair and mustache, the one-piece made Milos look more like an acrobat in a third-rate circus.

There was an excited babble of low-voiced reaction. Calvin said, "Well . . . shit." Colonel Flood gave a sharp nod, to say he agreed completely.

The bartender posed regally before Eric, who after a startled instant bowed before the much shorter vampire. "My lord," Eric said, "I am humbled. That you should honor us . . . that you should actually be here . . . on this day, of all days . . . I am overcome."

"Fucking poser," Pam muttered in my ear. She'd glided up behind me in the hubbub following the bartender's announcement.

"You think?" I was watching the spectacle of the confident and regal Eric babbling away, actually sinking down on one knee.

Dracula made a hushing gesture, and Eric's mouth snapped shut in midsentence. So did the mouths of every vamp in the place. "Since I have been here incognito for a week," Dracula said grandly, his accent harsh but not unattractive, "I have become so fond of this place that I propose to stay for a year. I will take your tribute while I am here, to live in the style I enjoyed during life. Though the bottled Royalty is acceptable as a stopgap, I, Dracula, do not care for this modern habit of drinking artificial blood, so I will require one woman a day. This one will do to start with." He pointed at me, and Colonel Flood and Calvin moved instantly to flank me, a gesture I appreciated. The vampires looked confused, an expression which didn't sit well on undead faces; except Bill. His face went completely blank.

Eric followed Vlad Tepes's stubby finger, identifying me as the future Happy Meal. Then he stared at Dracula, looking up from his kneeling position. I couldn't read his face at all, and I felt a stirring of fear. What would Charlie Brown have done if the Great Pumpkin wanted to eat the little red-haired girl?

"And as for my financial maintenance, a tithe from your club's income and a house will be sufficient for my needs, with some servants thrown in: your second-in-command, or your club manager, one of them should do. . . ." Pam actually growled, a low-level sound that made my hair stand up on my neck. Clancy looked as though someone had kicked his dog.

Pam was fumbling with the centerpiece of the table, hidden by my body. After a second, I felt something pressed into my hand. I glanced down. "You're the human," she whispered.

"Come, girl," Dracula said, beckoning with a curving of his fingers. "I hunger. Come to me and be honored before all these assembled."

Though Colonel Flood and Calvin both grabbed my arms, I said very softly, "This isn't worth your lives. They'll kill you if you try to fight. Don't worry," and I pulled away from them, meeting their eyes, in turn, as I spoke. I was trying to project confidence. I didn't know what they were getting, but they understood there was a plan.

I tried to glide toward the spangled bartender as if I were entranced. Since that's something vamps can't do to me, and Dracula obviously never doubted his own powers, I got away with it.

"Master, how did you escape from

your tomb at Târgovişte?" I asked, doing my best to sound admiring and dreamy. I kept my hands down by my sides so the folds of rosy chiffon would conceal them.

"Many have asked me that," the Dark Prince said, inclining his head graciously as Eric's own head jerked up, his brows drawn together. "But that story must wait. My beautiful one, I am so glad you left your neck bare tonight. Come closer to me . . . *ERRRK!*"

"*That's* for the bad dialogue!" I said, my voice trembling as I tried to shove the stake in even harder.

"And *that's* for the embarrassment," Eric said, giving the end a tap with his fist, just to help, as the "Prince" stared at us in horror. The stake obligingly disappeared into his chest.

"You dare . . . you dare," the short vampire croaked. "You shall be executed."

"I don't think so," I said. His face went blank, and his eyes were empty. Flakes began to drift from his skin as he crumpled.

But as the self-proclaimed Dracula sank to the floor and I looked around me, I wasn't so sure. Only the presence of Eric at my side kept the assemblage from falling on me and taking care of business. The vampires from out of town were the most dangerous; the vampires that knew me would hesitate.

"He wasn't Dracula," I said as clearly and loudly as I could. "He was an impostor."

"Kill her!" said a thin female vamp with short brown hair. "Kill the murderess!" She had a heavy accent, I thought Russian. I was about tired of the new wave of vamps.

Pot calling the kettle black, I thought briefly. I said, "You-all really think this goober was the Prince of Darkness?" I pointed to the flaking mess on the floor, held together by the spangled jumpsuit.

"He is dead. Anyone who kills Dracula must die," said Indira quietly, but not like she was going to rush over and rip my throat out.

"Any *vampire* who kills Dracula must die," Pam corrected. "But Sookie is not a vampire, and this was not Dracula."

"She killed one impersonating our founder," Eric said, making sure he could be heard throughout the club. "Milos was not the real Dracula. I would have staked him myself if I had had my wits about me." But I was standing right by Eric, my hand on his arm, and I knew he was shaking.

"How do you know that? How could she tell, a human who had only a few moments in his presence? He looked just like the woodcuts!" This from a tall, heavy man with a French accent.

"Vlad Tepes was buried at the monastery on Snagov," Pam said calmly, and everyone turned to her. "Sookie asked him how he'd escaped from his tomb at Târgovişte."

Well, that hushed them up, at least temporarily. I began to think I might live through this night.

"Recompense must be made to his maker," pointed out the tall, heavy vampire. He'd calmed down quite a bit in the last few minutes.

"If we can determine his maker," Eric said, "certainly."

"I'll search my database," Bill offered. He was standing in the shadows, where he'd lurked all evening. Now he took a step forward, and his dark eyes sought me out like a police helicopter searchlight catches the fleeing felon on *Cops.* "I'll find out his real name, if no one here has met him before."

All the vamps present glanced around. No one stepped forward to claim Milos/Dracula's acquaintance.

"In the meantime," Eric said smoothly, "let's not forget that this event should be a secret amongst us until we can find out more details." He smiled with a great show of fang, making his point quite nicely. "What happens in Shreveport, stays in Shreveport."

There was a murmur of assent.

"What do you say, guests?" Eric asked the non-vamp attendees.

Colonel Flood said, "Vampire business is not pack business. We don't care if you kill each other. We won't meddle in your affairs."

Calvin shrugged. "Panthers don't mind what you do."

The goblin said, "I've already forgotten the whole thing," and the madwoman beside him nodded and laughed. The few other non-vamps hastily agreed.

No one solicited my answer. I guess they were taking my silence for a given, and they were right.

Pam drew me aside. She made an annoyed sound, like *"tchk,"* and brushed at my dress. I looked down to see a fine spray of blood had misted across the chiffon skirt. I knew immediately that I'd never wear my beloved bargain dress again.

"Too bad, you look good in pink," Pam said.

I started to offer the dress to her, then thought again. I would wear it home and burn it. Vampire blood on my dress? Not a good piece of evidence to leave hanging around someone's closet. If experience has taught me anything, it's to dispose instantly of bloodstained clothing

"That was a brave thing you did," Pam said.

"Well, he was going to bite me," I said. "To death."

"Still," she said.

I didn't like the calculating look in

her eyes.

"Thank you for helping Eric when I couldn't," Pam said. "My maker is a big idiot about the prince."

"I did it because he was going to suck my blood," I told her.

"You did some research on Vlad Tepes."

"Yes, I went to the library after you told me about the original Dracula, and I Googled him."

Pam's eyes gleamed. "Legend has it that the original Vlad III was beheaded before he was buried."

"That's just one of the stories surrounding his death," I said.

"True. But you know that not even a vampire can survive a beheading."

"I would think not."

"So you know the whole thing may be a crock of shit."

"Pam," I said, mildly shocked. "Well, it might be. And it might not. After all, Eric talked to someone who said he was the real Dracula's gofer."

"You knew that Milos wasn't the real Dracula the minute he stepped forth."

I shrugged.

Pam shook her head at me. "You're too soft, Sookie Stackhouse. It'll be the death of you some day."

"Nah, I don't think so," I said. I was watching Eric, his golden hair falling forward as he looked down at the rapidly disintegrating remains of the self-styled Prince of Darkness. The thousand years of his life sat on him heavily, and for a second I saw every one of them. Then, by degrees, his face lightened, and when he looked up at me, it was with the expectancy

of a child on Christmas Eve.
"Maybe next year," he said.

■ ■ ■ ■

ONE WORD
ANSWER

■ ■ ■ ■

Bubba the Vampire and I were raking up clippings from my newly trimmed bushes about midnight when the long black car pulled up. I'd been enjoying the gentle scent of the cut bushes and the songs of the crickets and frogs celebrating spring. Everything hushed with the arrival of the black limousine. Bubba vanished immediately, because he didn't recognize the car. Since he changed over to the vampire persuasion, Bubba's been on the shy side.

I leaned against my rake, trying to

look nonchalant. In reality, I was far from relaxed. I live pretty far out in the country, and you have to want to be at my house to find the way. There's not a sign out at the parish road that points down my driveway reading STACKHOUSE HOME. My home is not visible from the road, because the driveway meanders through some woods to arrive in the clearing where the core of the house has stood for a hundred and sixty years.

Visitors are not real frequent, and I didn't remember ever seeing a limousine before. No one got out of the long black car for a couple of minutes. I began to wonder if maybe I should have hidden myself, like Bubba. I had the outside lights on, of course, since I couldn't see in the dark like Bubba, but the limousine windows were heavily smoked. I was real tempted to whack the shiny bumper with my rake to find out what would happen. Fortunately, the door opened while I was still thinking about it.

A large gentleman emerged from the rear of the limousine. He was six feet tall, and he was made up of circles. The largest circle was his belly. The round head above it was almost bald, but a fringe of black hair circled it right above his ears. His little eyes were round, too, and black as his hair and his suit. His shirt was gleaming white, but his tie was black without a pattern. He looked like the director of a funeral home for the criminally insane.

"Not too many people do their yard

work at midnight," he commented, in a surprisingly melodious voice. The true answer — that I liked to rake when I had someone to talk to, and I had company that night with Bubba, who couldn't come out in the sunlight — was better left unsaid. I just nodded. You couldn't argue with his statement.

"Would you be the woman known as Sookie Stackhouse?" asked the large gentleman. He said it as if he often addressed creatures that weren't men or women, but something else entirely.

"Yes, sir, I am," I said politely. My grandmother, God rest her soul, had raised me well. But she hadn't raised a fool; I wasn't about to invite him in. I wondered why the driver didn't get out.

"Then I have a legacy for you."

"Legacy" meant someone had died. I didn't have anyone left except for my brother, Jason, and he was sitting down at Merlotte's Bar with his girlfriend, Crystal. At least that's where he'd been when I'd gotten off my barmaid's job a couple of hours before.

The little night creatures were beginning to make their sounds again, having decided the big night creatures weren't going to attack.

"A legacy from who?" I said. What makes me different from other people is that I'm telepathic. Vampires, whose minds are simply silent holes in a world made noisy to me by the cacophony of human brains, make restful companions for me, so I'd been enjoying Bubba's chatter. Now

I needed to rev up my gift. This wasn't a casual drop-in. I opened my mind to my visitor. While the large, circular gentleman was wincing at my ungrammatical question, I attempted to look inside his head. Instead of a stream of ideas and images (the usual human broadcast), his thoughts came to me in bursts of static. He was a supernatural creature of some sort.

"Whom," I corrected myself, and he smiled at me. His teeth were very sharp.

"Do you remember your cousin Hadley?"

Nothing could have surprised me more than this question. I leaned the rake against the mimosa tree and shook the plastic garbage bag that we'd already filled. I put the plastic band around the top before I spoke,

I could only hope my voice wouldn't choke when I answered him. "Yes, I do." Though I sounded hoarse, my words were clear.

Hadley Delahoussaye, my only cousin, had vanished into the underworld of drugs and prostitution years before. I had her high school junior picture in my photo album. That was the last picture she'd had taken, because that year she'd run off to New Orleans to make her living by her wits and her body. My aunt Linda, her mother, had died of cancer during the second year after Hadley's departure.

"Is Hadley still alive?" I said, hardly able to get the words out.

"Alas, no," said the big man, absently polishing his black-framed glasses on a clean white handkerchief.

His black shoes gleamed like mirrors. "Your cousin Hadley is dead, I'm afraid." He seemed to relish saying it. He was a man — or whatever — who enjoyed the sound of his own voice.

Underneath the distrust and confusion I was feeling about this whole weird episode, I was aware of a sharp pang of grief. Hadley had been fun as a child, and we'd been together a lot, naturally. Since I'd been a weird kid, Hadley and my brother, Jason, had been the only children I'd had to play with for the most part. When Hadley hit puberty, the picture changed; but I had some good memories of my cousin.

"What happened to her?" I tried to keep my voice even, but I knew it wasn't.

"She was involved in an Unfortunate Incident," he said.

That was the euphemism for a vampire killing. When it appeared in newspaper reports, it usually meant that some vampire had been unable to restrain his bloodlust and had attacked a human. "A vampire killed her?" I was horrified.

"Ah, not exactly. Your cousin Hadley was the vampire. She got staked."

This was so much bad and startling news that I couldn't take it in. I held up a hand to indicate he shouldn't talk for a minute, while I absorbed what he'd said, bit by bit.

"What is your name, please?" I asked.

"Mr. Cataliades," he said. I repeated that to myself several times since it was a name I'd never encountered. Emphasis on the *tal,* I told myself. And a long *e*.

"Where might you hail from?"

"For many years, my home has been New Orleans."

New Orleans was at the other end of Louisiana from my little town, Bon Temps. Northern Louisiana is pretty darn different from southern Louisiana in several fundamental ways: it's the Bible Belt without the pizzazz of New Orleans; it's the older sister who stayed home and tended the farm while the younger sister went out partying. But it shares other things with the southern part of the state, too: bad roads, corrupt politics, and a lot of people, both black and white, who live right on the poverty line.

"Who drove you?" I asked pointedly, looking at the front of the car.

"Waldo," called Mr. Cataliades,

"the lady wants to see you."

I was sorry I'd expressed an interest after Waldo got out of the driver's seat of the limo and I'd had a look at him. Waldo was a vampire, as I'd already established in my own mind by identifying a typical vampire brain signature, which to me is like a photographic negative, one I "see" with my brain. Most vampires are good-looking or extremely talented in some way or another. Naturally, when a vamp brings a human over, the vamp's likely to pick a human who attracted him or her by beauty or some necessary skill. I didn't know who the heck had brought over Waldo, but I figured it was somebody crazy. Waldo had long, wispy white hair that was almost the same color as his skin. He was maybe five foot eight, but he looked taller because he was very thin. Waldo's eyes looked red under the light I'd had mounted on the electric pole. The vampire's face looked corpse white with a faint greenish tinge, and his skin was wrinkled. I'd never seen a vampire who hadn't been taken in the prime of life.

"Waldo," I said, nodding. I felt lucky to have had such long training in keeping my face agreeable. "Can I get you anything? I think I have some bottled blood. And you, Mr. Cataliades? A beer? Some soda?"

The big man shuddered and tried to cover it with a graceful half bow. "Much too hot for coffee or alcohol for me, but perhaps we'll take refreshments later." It was maybe sixty-two degrees, but Mr. Cataliades was indeed sweating, I noticed. "May we come in?" he asked.

"I'm sorry," I said, without a bit of apology in my voice. "I think not." I was hoping that Bubba had had the sense to rush across the little valley between our properties to fetch my nearest neighbor, my former lover Bill Compton, known to the residents of Bon Temps as Vampire Bill.

"Then we'll conduct our business out here in your yard," Mr. Cataliades said coldly. He and Waldo came around the body of the limousine. I felt uneasy when it wasn't between us anymore, but they kept their distance. "Miss Stackhouse, you are your cousin's sole heir."

I understood what he said, but I was incredulous. "Not my brother, Jason?" Jason and Hadley, both three years older than I, had been great buddies.

"No. In this document, Hadley says she called Jason Stackhouse once for help when she was very low on funds. He ignored her request, so she's ignoring him."

"When did Hadley get staked?" I was concentrating very hard on not getting any visuals. Since she was older than I by three years, Hadley had been a mere twenty-nine when she'd died. She'd been my physical opposite in most ways. I was robust and blond, she was thin and dark. I was strong, she was frail. She'd had big, thickly lashed brown eyes, mine were blue; and now, this strange man was telling me, she had closed those eyes for good.

"A month ago." Mr. Cataliades had

to think about it. "She died about a month ago."

"And you're just now letting me know?"

"Circumstances prevented."

I considered that.

"She died in New Orleans?"

"Yes. She was a handmaiden to the queen," he said, as though he were telling me she'd gotten her partnership at a big law firm or managed to buy her own business.

"The Queen of Louisiana," I said cautiously.

"I knew you would understand," he said, beaming at me. " 'This is a woman who knows her vampires,' I said to myself when I met you."

"She knows this vampire," Bill said, appearing at my side in that disconcerting way he had.

A flash of displeasure went across Mr. Cataliades's face like quick lightning across the sky.

"And you would be?" he asked with cold courtesy.

"I would be Bill Compton, resident of this parish and friend to Miss Stackhouse," Bill said ominously. "I'm also an employee of the queen, like you."

The queen had hired Bill so the computer database about vampires he was working on would be her property. Somehow, I thought Mr. Cataliades performed more personal services. He looked like he knew where all the bodies were buried, and Waldo looked like he had put them there.

Bubba was right behind Bill, and when he stepped out of Bill's shadow, for the first time I saw the vampire Waldo show an emotion. He was in awe.

"Oh, my gracious! Is this El—" Mr. Cataliades blurted.

"Yes," said Bill. He shot the two strangers a significant glance. "This is *Bubba*. The past upsets him very much." He waited until the two had nodded in understanding. Then he looked down at me. His dark brown eyes looked black in the stark shadows cast by the overhead lights. His skin had the pale gleam that said "vampire." "Sookie, what's happened?"

I gave him a condensed version of Mr. Cataliades's message. Since Bill and I had broken up when he was unfaithful to me, we'd been trying to establish some other workable relationship. He was proving to be a reliable friend, and I was grateful for his presence.

"Did the queen order Hadley's death?" Bill asked my visitors.

Mr. Cataliades gave a good impression of being shocked. "Oh, no!" he exclaimed. "Her Highness would never cause the death of someone she held so dear."

Okay, here came another shock. "Ah, what kind of dear . . . ? How dear did the queen hold my cousin?" I asked. I wanted to be sure I was interpreting the implication correctly.

Mr. Cataliades gave me an old-fashioned look. "She held Hadley dearly," he said.

Okay, I got it.

Every vampire territory had a king or queen, and with that title came power. But the Queen of Louisiana had extra status, since she was seated in New Orleans, which was the most popular city in the United States if you were one of the undead. Since vampire tourism now accounted for so much of the city's revenue, even the humans of New Orleans listened to the queen's wants and wishes, in an unofficial way. "If Hadley was such a big favorite of the queen's, who'd be fool enough to stake her?" I asked.

"The Fellowship of the Sun," said Waldo, and I jumped. The vampire had been silent so long, I'd assumed he wasn't ever going to speak. The vampire's voice was as creaky and peculiar as his appearance. "Do you know the city well?"

I shook my head. I'd only been to

the Big Easy once, on a school field trip.

"You are familiar, perhaps, with the cemeteries that are called the Cities of the Dead?"

I nodded. Bill said, "Yes," and Bubba muttered, "Uh-huh." Several cemeteries in New Orleans had aboveground crypts because the water table in southern Louisiana was too high to allow ordinary below-ground burials. The crypts look like small white houses, and they're decorated and carved in some cases, so these very old burial grounds are called the Cities of the Dead. The historic cemeteries are fascinating and sometimes dangerous. There are living predators to be feared in the Cities of the Dead, and tourists are cautioned to visit them in large, guided parties and to leave at the end of the day.

"Hadley and I had gone to St. Louis Number One that night, right after we rose, to conduct a ritual." Waldo's face looked quite expressionless. The thought that this man had been the chosen companion of my cousin, even if just for an evening's excursion, was simply astounding. "They leaped from behind the tombs around us. The Fellowship fanatics were armed with holy items, stakes, and garlic — the usual paraphernalia. They were stupid enough to have gold crosses."

The Fellowship refused to believe that all vampires could not be restrained by holy items, despite all the evidence. Holy items worked on the very old vampires, the ones who had been brought up to be devout believers. The newer vampires only suffered from crosses if they were silver. Silver would burn any vampire. Oh, a wooden cross might have an effect on a vamp — if it was driven through his heart.

"We fought valiantly, Hadley and I, but in the end, there were too many for us, and they killed Hadley. I escaped with some severe knife wounds." His paper white face looked more regretful than tragic.

I tried not to think about Aunt Linda and what she would have had to say about her daughter becoming a vampire. Aunt Linda would have been even more shocked by the circumstances of Hadley's death: by assassination, in a famous cemetery reeking of Gothic atmosphere, in the company of this grotesque creature. Of course, all these exotic trappings wouldn't have devastated Aunt Linda as much as the stark fact of Hadley's murder.

I was more detached. I'd written Hadley off long ago. I'd never thought I would see her again, so I had a little spare emotional room to think of other things. I still wondered, painfully, why Hadley hadn't come home to see us. She might have been afraid, being a young vampire, that her bloodlust would rise at an embarrassing time and she'd find herself yearning to suck on someone inappropriate. She might have been shocked by the change in her own nature; Bill had told me over and over that vampires were human no longer, that they were emotional

149

about different things than humans. Their appetites and their need for secrecy had shaped the older vampires irrevocably.

But Hadley had never had to operate under those laws; she'd been made vampire after the Great Revelation, when vampires had revealed their presence to the world.

And the post-puberty Hadley, the one I was less fond of, wouldn't have been caught dead or alive with someone like Waldo. Hadley had been popular in high school, and she'd certainly been human enough then to fall prey to all the teenage stereotypes. She'd been mean to kids who weren't popular, or she'd just ignored them. Her life had been completely taken up by her clothes and her makeup and her own cute self.

She'd been a cheerleader, until she'd started adopting the Goth image.

"You said you two were in the cemetery to perform a ritual. What ritual?" I asked Waldo, just to gain some time to think. "Surely Hadley wasn't a witch as well." I'd run across a werewolf witch before, but never a vampire spell caster.

"There are traditions among the vampires of New Orleans," Mr. Cataliades said carefully. "One of these traditions is that the blood of the dead can raise the dead, at least temporarily. For conversational purposes, you understand."

Mr. Cataliades certainly didn't have any throwaway lines. I had to think about every sentence that came out of his mouth. "Hadley wanted to talk to a dead person?" I asked, once I'd digested his latest bombshell.

"Yes," said Waldo, chipping in again. "She wanted to talk to Marie Laveau."

"The voodoo queen? Why?" You couldn't live in Louisiana and not know the legend of Marie Laveau, a woman whose magical power had fascinated both black and white people, at a time when black women had no power at all.

"Hadley thought she was related to her." Waldo seemed to be sneering.

Okay, now I knew he was making it up. "Duh! Marie Laveau was African-American, and my family is white," I pointed out.

"This would be through her father's side," Waldo said calmly.

Aunt Linda's husband, Carey Delahoussaye, had come from New Orleans, and he'd been of French descent. His family had been there for several generations. He'd bragged about it until my whole family had gotten sick of his pride. I wondered if Uncle Carey had realized that his Creole bloodline had been enriched by a little African-American DNA somewhere back in the day. I had only a child's memory of Uncle Carey, but I figured that piece of knowledge would have been his most closely guarded secret.

Hadley, on the other hand, would have thought being descended from the notorious Marie Laveau was really cool. I found myself giving Waldo a little more credence. Where Hadley would've gotten such information, I couldn't imagine. Of course, I also couldn't imagine her as a lover of women, but evidently that had been her choice. My cousin Hadley, the cheerleader, had become a vampire lesbian voodooienne. Who knew?

I felt glutted with information I hadn't had time to absorb, but I was anxious to hear the whole story. I gestured to the emaciated vampire to continue.

"We put the three X's on the tomb," Waldo said. "As people do. Voodoo devotees believe this ensures their wish will be granted. And then Hadley cut herself, and let the blood drip on the stone, and she called out the magic words."

"Abracadabra, please, and thank you," I said automatically, and Waldo glared at me.

"You ought not to make fun," he said. With some notable exceptions, vampires are not known for their senses of humor, and Waldo was definitely a serious guy. His red-rimmed eyes glared at me.

"Is this really a tradition, Bill?" I asked. I no longer cared if the two men from New Orleans knew I didn't trust them.

"Yes," Bill said. "I haven't ever tried it myself, because I think the dead should be left alone. But I've seen it done."

"Does it work?" I was startled.

"Yes. Sometimes."

"Did it work for Hadley?" I asked Waldo.

The vampire glared at me. "No," he hissed. "Her intent was not pure enough."

"And these fanatics, they were just hiding among the tombs, waiting to jump out at you?"

"Yes," Waldo said. "I told you."

"And you, with your vampire hearing and smell, you didn't know there were people in the cemetery around you?" To my left, Bubba stirred. Even a vamp as dim as the too hastily recruited Bubba could see the sense of my question.

"Perhaps I knew there were people," Waldo said haughtily, "but those cemeteries are popular at night with criminals and whores. I didn't distinguish which people were making the noises."

"Waldo and Hadley were both favorites of the queen," Mr. Cataliades said admonishingly. His tone suggested that any favorite of the queen's was above reproach. But that wasn't what his words were saying. I looked at him thoughtfully. At the same moment, I felt Bill shift beside me. We hadn't been soul mates, I guess, since our relationship hadn't worked out, but at odd moments we seemed to think alike, and this was one of those moments. I wished I could read Bill's mind for once — though the great recommendation of Bill as a lover had been that I couldn't. Telepaths don't have an easy time of it when it comes to love affairs. In fact, Mr. Cataliades was the only one on the scene who had a brain I could scan, and he was none too human.

I thought about asking him what he was, but that seemed kind of tacky. Instead, I asked Bubba if he'd round up some folding yard chairs so we could all sit down, and while that was being arranged, I went in the house and heated up some TrueBlood for the three vampires and iced some Mountain Dew for Mr. Cataliades, who professed himself to be delighted with the offer.

While I was in the house, standing in front of the microwave and staring at it like it was some kind of oracle, I thought of just locking the door and letting them all do what they would. I had an ominous sense of the way the night was going, and I was tempted to let it take its course without me. But Hadley had been my cousin. On a whim, I took her picture down from the wall to give it a closer look.

All the pictures my grandmother had hung were still up; despite her death, I continued to think of the house as hers. The first picture was of Hadley at age six, with one front tooth. She was holding a big drawing of a dragon. I hung it back beside the picture of Hadley at ten, skinny and pigtailed, her arms around Jason and me. Next to it was the picture taken by the reporter for the parish paper, when Hadley had been crowned Miss Teen Bon Temps. At fifteen, she'd been radiantly happy in her rented white sequined gown, glittering crown on her head, flowers in her arms. The last picture had been taken during Hadley's junior year. By then, Hadley had begun using drugs, and she was all Goth: heavy eye makeup, black hair, crimson lips. Uncle Carey had left Aunt Linda some years before this incarnation, moved back to his proud New Orleans family; and by the time Hadley left, too, Aunt Linda had begun feeling bad. A few months after Hadley ran away, we'd finally gotten my father's sister to go to a doctor, and he'd found the cancer.

In the years since then, I'd often wondered if Hadley had ever found out her mother was sick. It made a difference to me. If she'd known but hadn't come home, that was a horse of one color. If she'd never known, that was a horse of a different one. Now that I knew she had crossed over and become the living dead, I had a new option. Maybe Hadley had known, but she just hadn't cared.

I wondered who had told Hadley she might be descended from Marie Laveau. It must have been someone who'd done enough research to sound convincing, someone who'd studied Hadley enough to know how much she'd enjoy the piquancy of being related to such a notorious woman.

I carried the drinks outside on a tray, and we all sat in a circle on my old lawn furniture. It was a bizarre gathering: the strange Mr. Cataliades, a telepath, and three vampires — though one of those was as addled as a vampire can be and still call himself undead.

When I was seated, Mr. Cataliades passed me a sheaf of papers, and I peered at them. The outside light was good enough for raking but not really good for reading. Bill's eyes were twenty times stronger than mine, so I passed the papers over to him.

"Your cousin left you some money and the contents of her apartment," Bill said. "You're her executor, too."

I shrugged. "Okay," I said. I knew Hadley couldn't have had much. Vampires are pretty good at amassing nest eggs, but Hadley could only have been a vampire for a very few years.

Mr. Cataliades raised his nearly invisible brows. "You don't seem excited."

"I'm a little more interested in how Hadley met her death."

Waldo looked offended. "I've described the circumstances to you. Do you want a blow-by-blow account of the fight? It was unpleasant, I assure you."

I looked at him for a few moments. "What happened to you?" I asked. This was very rude, to ask someone what on earth had made him so weird-looking, but common sense told me that there was more to learn. I had an obligation to my cousin, an obligation unaffected by any legacy she'd left me. Maybe this was why Hadley had left me something in her will. She knew I'd ask questions, and God love my brother, he wouldn't.

Rage flashed across Waldo's features, and then it was like he'd wiped his face with some kind of emotion eraser. The paper white skin relaxed into calm lines and his eyes were calm. "When I was human, I was an albino," Waldo said stiffly, and I felt the knee-jerk horror of someone who's been unpardonably curious about a disability. Just as I was about to apologize, Mr. Cataliades intervened again.

"And, of course," the big man said smoothly, "he's been punished by the queen."

This time, Waldo didn't restrain his glare. "Yes," he said finally. "The queen immersed me in a tank for a few years."

"A tank of what?" I was all at sea.

"Saline solution," Bill said, very quietly. "I've heard of this punishment. That's why he's wrinkled, as you see."

Waldo pretended not to hear Bill's aside, but Bubba opened his mouth. "You're sure 'nuff wrinkled, man, but don't you worry. The chicks like a man who's different."

Bubba was a kind vampire and well-intentioned.

I tried to imagine being in a tank of seawater for years and years. Then I tried not to imagine it. I could only wonder what Waldo had done to merit such a punishment. "And you were a favorite?" I asked.

Waldo nodded, with a certain dignity. "I had that honor."

I hoped I'd never receive such an honor. "And Hadley was, too?"

Waldo's face remained placid, though a muscle twitched in his jaw. "For a time."

Mr. Cataliades said, "The queen was pleased with Hadley's enthusiasm and childlike ways. Hadley was only one of a series of favorites. Eventually, the queen's favor would have fallen on someone else, and Hadley would have had to carve out another place in the queen's entourage."

Waldo looked quite pleased at that

and nodded. "That's the pattern."

I couldn't get why I was supposed to care, and Bill made a small movement that he instantly stilled. I caught it out of the corner of my eye, and I realized Bill didn't want me to speak. Pooh on him; I hadn't been going to, anyway.

Mr. Cataliades said, "Of course, your cousin was a little different from her predecessors. Wouldn't you say, Waldo?"

"No," Waldo said. "In time, it would have been just like before." He seemed to bite his lip to stop himself from talking; not a smart move for a vampire. A red drop of blood formed, sluggishly. "The queen would have tired of her. I know it. It was the girl's youth, it was the fact that she was one of the new vampires who has never known the shadows. Tell our queen that, Cataliades, when you return to New Orleans. If you hadn't kept the privacy glass up the whole trip, I could have discussed this with you as I drove. You don't have to shun me, as though I were a leper."

Mr. Cataliades shrugged. "I didn't want your company," he said. "Now, we'll never know how long Hadley would have reigned as favorite, will we, Waldo?"

We were on to something here, and we were being goaded and prodded in that direction by Waldo's companion, Mr. Cataliades. I wondered why. For the moment, I'd follow his lead. "Hadley was real pretty," I said. "Maybe the queen would've given her a permanent position."

"Pretty girls glut the market," Waldo

said. "Stupid humans. They don't know what our queen can do to them."

"If she wants to," Bill murmured. "If this Hadley had a knack for delighting the queen, if she had Sookie's charm, then she might have been happy and favored for many years."

"And I guess you'd be out on your ass, Waldo," I said prosaically. "So tell me, were there really fanatics in the cemetery? Or just one skinny, white, wrinkled fanatic, jealous and desperate?"

Then, suddenly, we were all standing, all but Mr. Cataliades, who was reaching into the briefcase.

Before my eyes, Waldo turned into something even less human. His fangs ran out, and his eyes glowed red. He became even thinner, his body folding in on itself. Beside me, Bill and Bubba changed, too. I didn't want to look at them when they were angry. Seeing my friends change like that was even worse than seeing my enemies do it. Full fighting mode is just scary.

"You can't accuse a servant of the queen," Waldo said, and he actually hissed.

Then Mr. Cataliades proved himself capable of some surprises of his own, as if I'd doubted it. Moving quickly and lightly, he rose from his lawn chair and tossed a silver lariat around the vampire's head, large enough in circumference to circle Waldo's shoulders. With a grace that startled me, he drew it tight at the critical moment, pinning Waldo's arms to his sides.

I thought Waldo would go berserk, but the vampire surprised me by holding still. "You'll die for this," Waldo said to the big round man, and Mr. Cataliades smiled at him.

"I think not," he said. "Here, Miss Stackhouse."

He tossed something in my direction, and quicker than I could watch, Bill's hand shot out to intercept it. We both stared at what Bill was holding in his hand. It was polished, sharp, and wooden; a hardwood stake.

"What's up with this?" I asked Mr. Cataliades, moving closer to the long black limo.

"My dear Miss Stackhouse, the queen wanted you to have the pleasure."

Waldo, who had been glaring with

considerable defiance at everyone in the clearing, seemed to deflate when he heard what Mr. Cataliades had to say.

"She knows," the albino vampire said, and the only way I can describe his voice is "heartbroken." I shivered. He loved his queen, really loved her.

"Yes," the big man said, almost gently. "She sent Valentine and Charity to the cemetery immediately, when you rushed in with your news. They found no traces of human attack on what was left of Hadley. Only your smell, Waldo."

"She sent me here with you," Waldo said, almost whispering.

"Our queen wanted Hadley's kin to have the right of execution," Mr. Cataliades said.

I came closer to Waldo, until I was

as close as I could get. The silver had weakened the vampire, though I had a feeling that he wouldn't have struggled even if the chain hadn't been made of the metal that vampires can't tolerate. Some of the fire had gone out of Waldo, though his upper lip drew back from his fangs as I put the tip of the stake over his heart. I thought of Hadley, and I wondered, if she were in my shoes, could she do this?

"Can you drive the limo, Mr. Cataliades?" I asked.

"Yes, ma'am, I can."

"Could you drive yourself back to New Orleans?"

"That was always my plan."

I pressed down on the wood, until I could tell it was hurting him. His eyes were closed. I had staked a vampire before, but it had been to save my life and Bill's. Waldo was a pitiful thing. There was nothing romantic or dramatic about this vampire. He was simply vicious. I was sure he could do extreme damage when the situation called for it, and I was sure he had killed my cousin Hadley.

Bill said, "I'll do it for you, Sookie." His voice was smooth and cold, as always, and his hand on my arm was cool.

"I can help," Bubba offered. "You'd do it for me, Miss Sookie."

"Your cousin was a bitch and a whore," Waldo said, unexpectedly. I met his red eyes.

"I expect she was," I said. "I guess I just can't kill you." My hand, the one holding the stake, dropped to my side.

"You have to kill me," Waldo said, with the arrogance of surety. "The queen has sent me here to be killed."

"I'm just gonna have to ship you right back to the queen," I said. "I can't do it."

"Get your whoremonger to do it; he's more than willing."

Bill was looking more vampiric by the second, and he tugged the stake from my fingers.

"He's trying to commit suicide by cop, Bill," I said.

Bill looked puzzled, and so did Bubba. Mr. Cataliades's round face was unreadable.

"He's trying to make us mad enough, or scared enough, to kill him, because he can't kill himself," I said. "He's sure the queen will do something much, much worse to him than I would. And he's right."

"The queen was trying to give you the gift of vengeance," Mr. Cataliades said. "Won't you take it? She may not be happy with you if you send him back."

"That's really her problem," I said. "Isn't it?"

"I think it might be very much your problem," Bill said quietly.

"Well, that just bites," I said. "You . . ." I paused, and told myself not to be a fool. "You were very kind to bring Waldo down here, Mr. Cataliades, and you were very clever in steering me around to the truth." I took a deep breath and considered. "I appreciate your bringing down the legal papers, which I'll look over at a calmer moment." I thought I'd covered everything. "Now, if you'd be so good as to pop the trunk open, I'll ask Bill and Bubba to put him in there." I jerked my head toward the silver-bound vampire, standing in silence not a yard away.

At that moment, when we were all thinking of something else, Waldo threw himself at me, jaws open wide like a snake's, fangs fully extended. I threw myself backward, but I knew it wouldn't be enough. Those fangs would rip open my throat, and I would bleed out here in my own yard. But Bubba and Bill were not bound with silver, and with a speed that was terrifying in itself, they gripped the old vampire and knocked him to the ground. Quicker than any human could wink, Bill's arm rose and fell, and Waldo's red eyes looked down at the stake in his chest with profound satisfaction. In the next second, those eyes caved in and his long, thin body began the instant process of disintegration. You never have to bury a really dead vampire.

For a few long moments, we stayed frozen in the tableau; Mr. Cataliades was standing, I was on the ground on my butt, and Bubba and Bill were on their knees beside the thing that had been Waldo.

Then the limo door opened, and before Mr. Cataliades could scramble to help her out, the Queen of Louisiana stepped out of the vehicle.

She was beautiful, of course, but not in a fairy-tale princess sort of way. I don't know what I expected, but she wasn't it. While Bill and Bubba scrambled to their feet and then bowed deeply, I gave her a good once-over. She was wearing a very expensive midnight blue suit and high heels. Her hair was a rich reddish brown. Of course, she was pale as milk, but her eyes were large, tilted, and almost the same brown as her hair. Her fingernails were polished red, and somehow that seemed very weird. She wore no jewelry.

Now I knew why Mr. Cataliades had kept the privacy glass up during the trip north. And I was sure that the queen had ways of masking her presence from Waldo's senses, as well as his sight.

"Hello," I said uncertainly. "I'm . . ."

"I know who you are," she said. She had a faint accent; I thought it might be French. "Bill. Bubba."

Oooh-kay. So much for polite chitchat. I huffed out a breath and shut my mouth. No point in talking until she explained her presence. Bill and Bubba stood upright. Bubba was smiling. Bill wasn't.

The queen examined me head to toe, in a way I thought was downright rude. Since she was a queen, she was an old vampire, and the oldest ones, the ones who sought power in the vampire infrastructure, were among the scariest. It had been so long since she'd been human that there might not be much remembrance of humanity left in her.

"I don't see what all the fuss is about," she said, shrugging.

My lips twitched. I just couldn't help it. My grin spread across my face, and I tried to hide it with my hand. The queen eyed me quizzically.

"She smiles when she's nervous," Bill said.

I did, but that's not why I was smiling now.

"You were going to send Waldo back to me, for me to torture and kill," the queen said to me. Her face was quite blank. I couldn't tell if she approved or disapproved, thought I was clever or thought I was a fool.

"Yes," I said. The shortest answer was definitely the best.

"He forced your hand."

"Uh-huh."

"He was too frightened of me to risk returning to New Orleans with my friend Mr. Cataliades."

"Yes." I was getting good at one-word answers.

"I wonder if you engineered this whole thing."

"Yes" would not be the right answer here. I maintained silence.

"I'll find out," she said, with absolute certainty. "We'll meet again, Sookie Stackhouse. I was fond of your cousin, but even she was foolish enough to go to a cemetery alone with her bitterest enemy. She counted too much on the power of my name alone to protect her."

"Did Waldo ever tell you if Marie Laveau actually rose?" I asked, too overwhelmed with curiosity to let the question go unanswered.

She was getting back in the car as I spoke, and she paused with one foot inside the limo and one foot in the yard. Anyone else would have looked awkward, but not the Queen of Louisiana.

"Interesting," she said. "No, actually, he didn't. When you come to New Orleans, you and Bill can repeat the experiment."

I started to point out that unlike Hadley, I wasn't dead, but I had the sense to shut my mouth. She might have ordered me to become a vampire, and I was afraid, very afraid, that then Bill and Bubba would have held me down and made me so. That was too awful to think about, so I smiled at her.

After the queen was all settled in the limo, Mr. Cataliades bowed to me. "It's been a pleasure, Miss Stackhouse. If you have any questions about your cousin's estate, call me at the number on my business card. It's clipped to the papers."

"Thanks," I said, not trusting myself to say more. Besides, one-word answers never hurt. Waldo was almost disintegrated. Bits of him would be in my yard for a while. Yuck. "Where's Waldo? All over my yard," I could say to anyone who asked.

The night had clearly been too much for me. The limo purred out of my yard. Bill put his hand to my cheek, but I didn't lean into it. I was grateful to him for coming, and I told him so.

"You shouldn't be in danger," he said. Bill had a habit of using a word that changed the meaning of his statements, made them something ambiguous and unsettling. His dark eyes were fathomless pools. I didn't think I would ever understand him.

"Did I do good, Miss Sookie?" Bubba asked.

"You did great, Bubba," I said.

"You did the right thing without me even having to tell you."

"You knew all along she was in the limo," Bubba said. "Didn't you, Miss Sookie?"

Bill looked at me, startled. I didn't meet his eyes. "Yes, Bubba," I said gently. "I knew. Before Waldo got out, I listened with my other sense, and I found two blank spots in the limo." That could only mean two vampires. So I'd known Cataliades had had a companion in the back of the limousine.

"But you played it all out like she wasn't there." Bill couldn't seem to grasp this. Maybe he didn't think I'd learned anything since I'd met him. "Did you know ahead of time that Waldo would make a try for you?"

"I suspected he might. He didn't

want to go back to her mercies."

"So." Bill caught my arms and looked down at me. "Were you trying to make sure he died all along, or were you trying to send him back to the queen?"

"Yes," I said.

One-word answers never hurt.

■ ■ ■ ■

LUCKY

■ ■ ■ ■

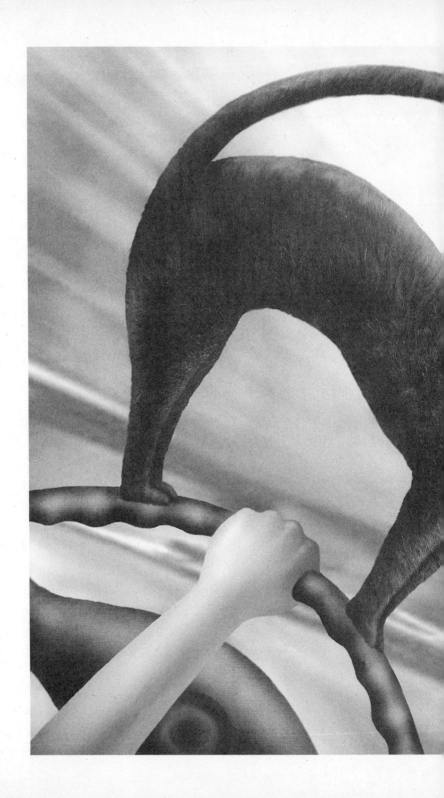

Amelia Broadway and I were painting each other's toenails when my insurance agent knocked at the front door. I'd picked Roses on Ice. Amelia had opted for Mad Burgundy Cherry Glacé. She'd finished my feet, and I had about three toes to go on her left foot when Greg Aubert interrupted us.

Amelia had been living with me for months, and it had been kind of nice to have someone else sharing my old house. Amelia is a witch from New Orleans, and she had been staying with me because she'd had a magical misfortune she didn't want any of her witch buddies in the Big Easy to know about. Also, since Katrina, she really doesn't have anything to go home to, at least for a while. My little hometown of Bon Temps was swollen with refugees.

Greg Aubert had been to my house after I'd had a fire that caused a lot of damage. As far as I knew, I didn't have any insurance needs at the moment. I was pretty curious about his purpose, I confess.

Amelia had glanced up at Greg, found his sandy hair and rimless glasses uninteresting, and completed painting her little toe while I ushered him to the wingback chair.

"Greg, this is my friend Amelia Broadway," I said. "Amelia, this is

Greg Aubert."

Amelia looked at Greg with more interest. I'd told her Greg was a colleague of hers, in some respects. Greg's mom had been a witch, and he'd found using the craft very helpful in protecting his clients. Not a car got insured with Greg's agency without having a spell cast on it. I was the only one in Bon Temps who knew about Greg's little talent. Witchcraft wouldn't be popular in our devout little town. Greg always handed his clients a lucky rabbit's foot to keep in their new vehicles or homes.

After he turned down the obligatory offer of iced tea or water or Coke, Greg sat on the edge of the chair while I resumed my seat on one end of the couch. Amelia had the other end.

"I felt the wards when I drove up," Greg told Amelia. "Very impressive." He was trying real hard to keep his eyes off my tank top. I would have put on a bra if I'd known we were going to have company.

Amelia tried to look indifferent, and she might have shrugged if she hadn't been holding a bottle of nail polish. Amelia, tan and athletic, with short glossy brown hair, is not only pleased with her looks but really proud of her witchcraft abilities. "Nothing special," she said, with unconvincing modesty. She smiled at Greg, though.

"What can I do for you today, Greg?" I asked. I was due to go to work in an hour, and I had to change and pull my long hair up in a ponytail.

"I need your help," he said, yanking

his gaze up to my face.

No beating around the bush with Greg.

"Okay, how?" If he could be direct, so could I.

"Someone's sabotaging my agency," he said. His voice was suddenly passionate, and I realized Greg was really close to a major breakdown. He wasn't quite the broadcaster Amelia was — I could read most thoughts Amelia had as clearly as if she'd spoken them — but I could certainly read his inner workings.

"Tell us about it," I said, because Amelia could not read Greg's mind.

"Oh, thanks," he said, as if I'd agreed to do something. I opened my mouth to correct this idea, but he plowed ahead.

"Last week I came into the office to

find that someone had been through the files."

"You still have Marge Barker working for you?"

He nodded. A stray beam of sunlight winked off his glasses. It was October, and still warm in northern Louisiana. Greg got out a snowy handkerchief and patted his forehead. "I've got my wife, Christy; she comes in three days a week for half a day. And I've got Marge full-time." Christy, Greg's wife, was as sweet as Marge was sour.

"How'd you know someone had been through the files?" Amelia asked. She screwed on the top of the polish bottle and put it on the coffee table.

Greg took a deep breath. "I'd been thinking for a couple of weeks that someone had been in the office at night. But nothing was missing. Nothing was changed. My wards were okay. But two days ago, I got into the office to find that one of the drawers on our main filing cabinet was open. Of course, we lock them at night," he said. "We've got one of those filing systems that locks up when you turn a key in the top drawer. Almost all of the client files were at risk. But every day, last thing in the afternoon, Marge goes around and locks all the cabinets. What if someone suspects . . . what I do?"

I could see how that would shiver Greg down to his liver. "Did you ask Marge if she remembered locking the cabinet?"

"Sure I asked her. She got mad — you know Marge — and said she definitely did. My wife had worked that afternoon, but she couldn't remember if she watched Marge lock the cabinets or not. And Terry Bellefleur had dropped by at the last minute, wanting to check again on the insurance for his damn dog. He might have seen Marge lock up."

Greg sounded so irritated that I found myself defending Terry. "Greg, Terry doesn't like being the way he is, you know," I said, trying to gentle my voice. "He got messed up fighting for our country, and we got to cut him some slack."

Greg looked grumpy for a minute. Then he relaxed. "I know, Sookie," he said. "He's just been so hyped up about this dog."

"What's the story?" Amelia asked. If I have moments of curiosity,

Amelia has an imperative urge. She wants to know everything about everybody. The telepathy should have gone to her, not me. She might actually have enjoyed it, instead of considering it a disability.

"Terry Bellefleur is Andy's cousin," I said. I knew Amelia had met Andy, a police detective, at Merlotte's. "He comes in after closing and cleans the bar. Sometimes he substitutes for Sam. Maybe not the few evenings you were working." Amelia filled in at the bar from time to time.

"Terry fought in Vietnam, got captured, and had a pretty bad time of it. He's got scars inside and out. The story about the dogs is this: Terry loves hunting dogs, and he keeps buying himself these expensive Catahoulas, and things keep happening to them. His current bitch has had puppies. He's just on pins and needles lest something happen to her and the babies."

"You're saying Terry is a little unstable?"

"He has bad times," I said. "Sometimes he's just fine."

"Oh," Amelia said, and a lightbulb might as well have popped on above her head. "He's the guy with the long graying auburn hair, going bald at the front? Scars on his cheek? Big truck?"

"That's him," I said.

Amelia turned to Greg. "You said for at least a couple of weeks you'd felt someone had been in the building after it closed. That couldn't be your wife, or this Marge?"

"My wife is with me all evening unless we have to take the kids to different events. And I don't know why Marge would feel she had to come back at night. She's there during the day, every day, and often by herself. Well, the spells that protect the building seem okay to me. But I keep recasting them."

"Tell me about your spells," Amelia said, getting down to her favorite part.

She and Greg talked spells for a few minutes, while I listened but didn't comprehend. I couldn't even understand their thoughts.

Then Amelia said, "What do you want, Greg? I mean, why did you come to us?"

He'd actually come to me, but it was kind of nice to be an "us."

Greg looked from Amelia to me, and said, "I want Sookie to find out who opened my files, and why. I worked hard to become the bestselling Pelican State agent in northern Louisiana, and I don't want my business fouled up now. My son's about to go to Rhodes in Memphis, and it ain't cheap."

"Why are you coming to me instead of the police?"

"I don't want anyone else finding out what I am," he said, embarrassed but determined. "And it might come up if the police start looking into things at my office. Plus, you know, Sookie, I got you a real good payout on your kitchen."

My kitchen had been burned down by an arsonist months before. I'd just finished getting it all rebuilt. "Greg, that's your job," I said. "I don't see where the gratitude comes in."

"Well, I have a certain amount of discretion in arson cases," he said. "I could have told the home office that I thought you did it yourself."

"You wouldn't have done that," I said calmly, though I was seeing a side of Greg I didn't like. Amelia practically had flames coming out of her nose, she was so incensed. But I could tell that Greg was already ashamed of bringing up the possibility.

"No," he said, looking down at his hands. "I guess I wouldn't. I'm sorry I said that, Sookie. I'm scared someone'll tell the whole town what I do, why people I insure are so . . . lucky. Can you see what you can find out?"

"Bring your family into the bar for supper tonight, give me a chance to look them over," I said. "That's the real reason you want me to find out, right? You suspect your family might be involved. Or your staff."

He nodded, and he looked wretched.

"I'll try to get in there tomorrow to talk to Marge. I'll say you wanted me to drop by."

"Yeah, I make calls from my cell phone sometimes, ask people to come in," he said. "Marge would believe it."

Amelia said, "What can I do?"

"Well, can you be with her?" Greg said. "Sookie can do things you can't, and vice versa. Maybe between the two of you . . ."

"Okay," Amelia said, giving Greg the benefit of her broad and dazzling smile. Her dad must have paid dearly for the perfect white smile of Amelia Broadway, witch and waitress.

Bob the cat padded in just at that moment, as if belatedly realizing we had a guest. Bob jumped on the chair right beside Greg and examined him with care.

Greg looked down at Bob just as intently. "Have you been doing something you shouldn't, Amelia?"

"There's nothing strange about Bob," Amelia said, which was not true. She scooped up the black-and-white cat in her arms and nuzzled his soft fur. "He's just a big ole cat. Aren't you, Bob?" She was relieved when Greg dropped the subject. He got up to leave.

"I'll be grateful for anything you can do to help me," he said. With an abrupt switch to his professional persona, he said, "Here, have an extra lucky rabbit's foot," and reached in his pocket to hand me a lump of fake fur.

"Thanks," I said, and decided to put it in my bedroom. I could use some luck in that direction.

After Greg left, I scrambled into my work clothes (black pants and white boatneck T-shirt with MERLOTTE'S embroidered over the left breast), brushed my long blond hair and secured it in a ponytail, and left for the bar, wearing Teva sandals to show off my beautiful toenails. Amelia, who wasn't scheduled to work that night, said she might go have a good look around the insurance agency.

"Be careful," I said. "If someone really is prowling around there, you don't want to run into a bad situation."

"I'll zap 'em with my wonderful witch powers," she said, only half-joking. Amelia had a fine opinion of her own abilities, which led to mistakes like Bob. He had actually been a thin young witch, handsome in a nerdy way. While spending the night with Amelia, Bob had been the victim of one of her less successful attempts at major magic. "Besides, who'd want to break into an insurance agency?" she said quickly, having read the doubt on my face. "This whole thing is ridiculous. I do want to check out Greg's magic, though, and see if it's been tampered with."

"You can do that?"

"Hey, standard stuff."

■ ■ ■ ■

To my relief, the bar was quiet that night. It was Wednesday, which is never a very big day at supper time, since lots of Bon Temps citizens go to church on Wednesday night. Sam Merlotte, my boss, was busy counting cases of beer in the storeroom when I got there; that was how light the crowd was. The waitresses on duty were mixing their own drinks.

I stowed my purse in the drawer in Sam's desk that he keeps empty for them, then went out front to take over my tables. The woman I was relieving, a Katrina evacuee I hardly knew, gave me a wave and departed.

After an hour, Greg Aubert came in with his family as he'd promised. You seated yourself at Merlotte's, and

I surreptitiously nodded to a table in my section. Dad, Mom, and two teenagers, the nuclear family. Greg's wife, Christy, had medium-light hair like Greg, and like Greg she wore glasses. She had a comfortable middle-aged body, and she'd never seemed exceptional in any way. Little Greg (and that's what they called him) was about three inches taller than his father, about thirty pounds heavier, and about ten IQ points smarter. That is, book smart. Like most nineteen-year-olds, he was pretty dumb about the world. Lindsay, the daughter, had lightened her hair five shades and squeezed herself into an outfit at least a size too small, and could hardly wait to get away from her folks so she could meet the Forbidden Boyfriend.

While I took their drink and food orders, I discovered that (a) Lindsay had the mistaken idea that she looked like Christina Aguilera, (b) Little Greg thought he would never go into insurance because it was so boring, and (c) Christy thought Greg might be interested in another woman because he'd been so distracted lately. As you can imagine, it takes a lot of mental doing to separate what I'm getting from people's minds from what I'm hearing directly from their mouths, which accounts for the strained smile I often wear — the smile that's led some people to think I'm just crazy.

After I'd brought them their drinks and turned in their food order, I puttered around studying the Aubert family. They seemed so typical it just hurt. Little Greg thought about his girlfriend mostly, and I learned more than I wanted to know.

Greg was just worried.

Christy was thinking about the dryer in their laundry room, wondering if it was time to get a new one.

See? Most people's thoughts are like that. Christy was also weighing Marge Barker's virtues (efficiency, loyalty) against the fact that she seriously disliked the woman.

Lindsay was thinking about her secret boyfriend. Like teenage girls everywhere, she was convinced her parents were the most boring people in the universe and had pokers up their asses besides. They didn't understand *anything.* Lindsay herself didn't understand why Dustin wouldn't take her to meet his folks, why he wouldn't let her see where he lived. No one but Dustin knew how poetic her soul was, how fascinating she truly could be, how misunderstood she was.

If I had a dime for every time I'd heard that from a teenager's brain, I'd be as rich as John Edward, the psychic.

I heard the bell ding in the service window, and I trotted over to get the Auberts' order from our current cook. I loaded my arms with the plates and hustled them over to the table. I had to endure a full-body scan from Little Greg, but that was par for the course, too. Guys can't help it. Lindsay didn't register me at all. She was wondering why Dustin was so secretive about his daytime activities. Shouldn't he be in school?

Okay, now. We were getting some-where.

But then Lindsay began thinking about her D in algebra and how she was going to get grounded when her parents found out and then she wouldn't get to see Dustin for a while unless she climbed out of her bed-room window at two in the morning. She was seriously considering going all the way.

Lindsay made me feel sad and old. And very smart.

By the time the Aubert family paid their bill and left, I was tired of all of them, and my head was exhausted (a weird feeling, and one I simply can't describe).

I plodded through work the rest of the night, glad to the very ends of my Roses on Ice toenails when I headed out the back door.

"Psst," said a voice from behind me while I was unlocking my car door.

With a stifled shriek, I swung around with my keys in my hand, ready to attack.

"It's me," Amelia said gleefully.

"Dammit, Amelia, don't sneak up on me like that!" I sagged against the car.

"Sorry," she said, but she didn't sound very sorry. "Hey," she continued, "I've been over by the insurance agency. Guess what!"

"What?" My lack of enthusiasm seemed to register with Amelia.

"You tired or something?" she asked.

"I just had an evening of listening in on the world's most typical family," I said. "Greg's worried, Christy's worried, Little Greg is horny, and Lindsay has a secret love."

"I know," Amelia said. "And guess what?"

"He might be a vamp."

"Oh." She sagged. "You already knew?"

"Not for sure. I know other fascinating stuff, though. I know he understands Lindsay as she's never been understood before in her whole underappreciated life, that he just might be The One, and that she's thinking of having sex with this goober."

"Well, I know where he lives. Let's go by there. You drive; I need to get some stuff ready." We got into Amelia's car. I took the driver's seat. Amelia began fumbling in her purse through the many little Ziplocs that filled it. They were all full of magic ready to go: herbs and other ingredients. Bat wings, for all I knew.

"He lives by himself in a big house with a FOR SALE sign in the front yard. No furniture. Yet he looks like he's eighteen." Amelia pointed at the house, which was dark and isolated.

"Hmmm." Our eyes met.

"What do you think?" Amelia asked.

"Vampire, almost surely."

"Could be. But why would a strange vampire be in Bon Temps? Why don't any of the other vamps know about him?" It was all right to be a vampire in today's America, but the vamps were still trying to keep a low profile. They regulated themselves rigorously.

"How do you know they don't?

Know about him, that is."

Good question. Would the area vampires be obliged to tell me? It wasn't like I was an official vampire greeter or anything.

"Amelia, you went looking around after a vampire? Not smart."

"It wasn't like I knew he might be fangy when I started. I just followed him after I saw him cruising around the Auberts' house."

"I think he's in the middle of seducing Lindsay," I said. "I better make a call."

"But does this have anything to do with Greg's business?"

"I don't know. Where is this boy now?"

"He's at Lindsay's house. He finally just parked outside. I guess he's waiting for her to come out."

"Crap." I pulled in a little way down the street from the Auberts' ranch style. I flipped open my cell phone to call Fangtasia. Maybe it's not a good sign when the area vampire bar is on your speed dial.

"Fangtasia, the bar with a bite," said an unfamiliar voice. Just as Bon Temps and our whole area was saturated with human evacuees, the vampire community in Shreveport was, too.

"This is Sookie Stackhouse. I need to speak with Eric, please," I said.

"Oh, the telepath. Sorry, Miss Stackhouse. Eric and Pam are out tonight."

"Maybe you can tell me if any of the new vampires are staying in my town, Bon Temps?"

"Let me inquire."

The voice was back after a few minutes. "Clancy says no." Clancy was like Eric's third-in-command, and I was not his favorite person. You'll notice Clancy didn't even ask the phone guy to find out why I needed to know. I thanked the unknown vampire for his trouble and hung up.

I was stumped. Pam, Eric's second-in-command, was sort of a buddy of mine, and Eric was, occasionally, something more than that. Since they weren't there, I'd have to call our local vampire, Bill Compton.

I sighed. "I'm going to have to call Bill," I said, and Amelia knew enough of my history to understand why the idea was so traumatic. And then I braced myself and dialed.

"Yes?" said a cool voice.

Thank goodness. I'd been scared the new girlfriend, Selah, would answer.

"Bill, this is Sookie. Eric and Pam are out of touch, and I have a problem."

"What?"

Bill has always been a man of few words.

"There's a young man in town we think is a vampire. Have you met him?"

"Here in Bon Temps?" Bill was clearly surprised and displeased.

That answered my question. "Yes, and Clancy told me they hadn't farmed out any new vamps to Bon Temps. So I thought maybe you'd encountered this individual?"

"No, which means he's probably taking care not to cross my path.

Where are you?"

"We're parked outside the Auberts' house. He's interested in the daughter, a teenager. We've pulled into the driveway of a house for sale across the street, middle of the block on Hargrove."

"I'll be there very soon. Don't approach him."

As if I would. "He thinks I'm stupid enough —" I began, and Amelia already had her "Indignant for You" face on when the driver's door was yanked open and a white hand latched onto my shoulder. I squawked until the other hand clamped over my mouth.

"Shut up, breather," said a voice that was even colder than Bill's. "Are you the one that's been following me around all night?"

Then I realized that he didn't know Amelia was in the passenger's seat. That was good.

Since I couldn't speak, I nodded slightly.

"Why?" he growled. "What do you want with me?" He shook me like I was a dustcloth, and I thought all my bones would come disjointed.

Then Amelia leaped from the other side of the car and darted over to us, tossing the contents of a Ziploc on his head. Of course, I had no idea what she was saying, but the effect was dramatic. After a jolt of astonishment, the vampire froze. The problem was, he froze with me clasped with my back to his chest in an unbreakable hold. I was mashed against him, and his left hand was still hard over my mouth, his right hand around my waist. So far, the investigative team of Sookie Stackhouse, telepath, and Amelia Broadway, witch, was not doing a top-flight job.

"Pretty good, huh?" Amelia said.

I managed to move my head a fraction. "Yes, if I could breathe," I said. I wished I hadn't wasted breath speaking.

Then Bill was there, surveying the situation.

"You stupid woman, Sookie's trapped," Bill said. "Undo the spell."

Under the streetlight, Amelia looked sullen. Undoing was not her best thing, I realized with some anxiety. I couldn't do anything else, so I waited while she worked on the counterspell.

"If this doesn't work, it'll only take me a second to break his arm," Bill told me. I nodded . . . well, I moved my head a fraction of an inch . . . because that was all I could do. I was getting pretty breathless.

Suddenly there was a little *pop!* in the air, and the younger vampire let go of me to launch himself at Bill — who wasn't there. Bill was behind him, and he grabbed one of the boy's arms and twisted it up and back. The boy screamed, and down they went to the ground. I wondered if anyone was going to call the police. This was a lot of noise and activity for a residential neighborhood after one o'clock. But no lights came on.

"Now, talk." Bill was absolutely determined, and I guess the boy knew it.

"What's your problem?" the boy demanded. He had spiked brown hair and a lean build and a couple of diamond studs in his nose. "This woman's been following me around. I need to know who she is."

Bill looked up at me questioningly. I jerked my head toward Amelia.

"You didn't even grab the right woman," Bill said. He sounded kind of disappointed in the youngster. "Why are you here in Bon Temps?"

"Getting away from Katrina," the boy said. "My sire was staked by a human when we ran out of bottled blood substitute after the flood. I stole a car outside of New Orleans, changed the license plates, and got out of town. I reached here at day-light. I found an empty house with a FOR SALE sign and a windowless bathroom, so I moved in. I've been going out with a local girl. I take a sip every night. She's none the wiser," he sneered.

"What's your interest?" Bill asked me.

"Have you two been going into her dad's office at night?" I asked.

"Yeah, once or twice." He smirked. "Her dad's office has a couch in it." I wanted to slap the shit out of him, maybe smacking the jewelry in his nose just by accident.

"How long have you been a vampire?" Bill asked.

"Ah . . . maybe two months."

Okay, that explained a lot. "So that's why he didn't know to check in with Eric. That's why he doesn't realize what he's doing is foolish and liable to get him staked."

"There's only so much excuse for stupidity," Bill said.

"Have you gone through the files in there?" I asked the boy, who was looking a little dazed.

"What?"

"Did you go through the files in the insurance office?"

"Uh, no. Why would I do that? I was just loving up the girl, to get a little sip, you know? I was real careful not to take too much. I don't have any money to buy artificial stuff."

"Oh, you are *so dumb.*" Amelia was fed up with this kid. "For goodness' sake, learn something about your condition. Stranded vampires can get help just like stranded people. You just ask the Red Cross for some synthetic blood, and they dole it out free."

"Or you could have found out who the sheriff of the area is," Bill said.

"Eric would never turn away a vampire in need. What if someone had found you biting this girl? She's under the age of consent, I gather?" For blood "donation" to a vampire.

"Yeah," I said, when Dustin looked blank. "It's Lindsay, daughter of Greg Aubert, my insurance agent. He wanted us to find out who'd been going into his building at night. Called in a favor to get me and Amelia to investigate."

"He should do his own dirty work," Bill said quite calmly. But his hands were clenched. "Listen, boy, what's your name?"

"Dustin." He'd even given Lindsay his real name.

"Well, Dustin, tonight we go to Fangtasia, the bar in Shreveport that Eric Northman uses as his headquarters. He will talk to you there, decide what to do with you."

"I'm a free vampire. I go where I want."

"Not within Area Five, you don't. You go to Eric, the area sheriff."

Bill marched the young vampire off into the night, probably to load him into his car and get him to Shreveport.

Amelia said, "I'm sorry, Sookie."

"At least you stopped him from breaking my neck," I said, trying to sound philosophical about it. "We still have our original problem. It wasn't Dustin who went through the files, though I'm guessing it was Dustin and Lindsay going into the office at night that disturbed the magic. How could they get past it?"

"After Greg told me his spell, I realized he wasn't much of a witch. Lindsay's a member of the family. With Greg's spell to ward against outsiders, that made a difference," Amelia said. "And sometimes vampires register as a void on spells created for humans. After all, they're not alive. I made my 'freeze' spell vampire specific."

"Who else can get through magic spells and work mischief?"

"Magical nulls," she said.

"Huh?"

"There are people who can't be affected by magic," Amelia said. "They're rare, but they exist. I've only met one before."

"How can you detect nulls? Do they give off a special vibration or something?"

"Only very experienced witches can

detect nulls without casting a spell on them that fails," Amelia admitted. "Greg probably has never encountered one."

"Let's go see Terry," I suggested. "He stays up all night."

The baying of a dog announced our arrival at Terry's cabin. Terry lived in the middle of three acres of woods. Terry liked being by himself most of the time, and any social needs he might feel were satisfied by an occasional stint of working as a bartender.

"That'll be Annie," I said, as the barking rose in intensity. "She's his fourth."

"Wife? Or dog?"

"Dog. Specifically, a Catahoula. The first one got hit by a truck, I think, and one got poisoned, and one got bit by a snake."

"Gosh, that is bad luck."

"Yeah, unless it's not chance at all. Maybe someone's making it happen."

"What are Catahoulas for?"

"Hunting. Herding. Don't get Terry started on the history of the breed, I'm begging you."

Terry's trailer door opened, and Annie launched herself off the steps to find out if we were friends or foes. She gave us a good bark, and when we stayed still, she eventually remembered she knew me. Annie weighed about fifty pounds, I guess, a good-sized dog. Catahoulas are not beautiful unless you love the breed. Annie was several shades of brown and red, and one shoulder was a solid color while her legs were another, though her rear half was covered with spots.

"Sookie, did you come to pick out a puppy?" Terry called. "Annie, let them by." Annie obediently backed up, keeping her eyes on us as we began approaching the trailer.

"I came to look," I said. "I brought my friend Amelia. She loves dogs."

Amelia was thinking she'd like to slap me upside the head because she was definitely a cat person.

Annie's puppies and Annie had made the small trailer quite doggy, though the odor wasn't really unpleasant. Annie herself maintained a vigilant stance while we looked at the three pups Terry still had. Terry's scarred hands were gentle as he handled the dogs. Annie had encountered several gentleman dogs on her unplanned excursion, and the puppies were diverse. They were adorable. Puppies just are. But they were sure distinctive. I picked up a bundle of short reddish fur with a white muzzle, and felt the puppy wiggle against me and snuffle my fingers. Gee, it was cute.

"Terry," I said, "have you been worried about Annie?"

"Yeah," he said. Since he was off base himself, Terry was very tolerant of other people's quirks. "I got to thinking about the things that have happened to my dogs, and I began to wonder if someone was causing them all."

"Do you insure all your dogs with Greg Aubert?"

"Naw, Diane at Liberty South insured the others. And see what happened to them? I decided to switch agents, and everyone says Greg is the luckiest son of a bitch in Renard Parish."

The puppy began chewing on my fingers. Ouch. Amelia was looking around her at the dingy trailer. It was clean enough, but the furniture arrangement was strictly utilitarian, like the furniture itself.

"So, did you go through the files at Greg Aubert's office?"

"No, why would I do that?"

Truthfully, I couldn't think of a reason. Fortunately, Terry didn't seem interested in why I wanted to know. "Sookie," he said, "if anyone in the bar thinks about my dogs, knows anything about 'em, will you tell me?"

Terry knew about me. It was one of those community secrets that everyone knows but no one ever discusses.

Until they need me.

"Yes, Terry, I will." It was a promise, and I shook his hand. Reluctantly, I set the puppy back in its improvised pen, and Annie checked it over anxiously to make sure it was in good order.

We left soon after, none the wiser.

"So, who've we got left?" Amelia said. "You don't think the family did it, the vampire boyfriend is cleared, and Terry, the only other person on the scene, didn't do it. Where do we look next?"

"Don't you have some magic that would give us a clue?" I asked. I pictured us throwing magic dust on the files to reveal fingerprints.

"Uh. No."

"Then let's just reason our way through it. Like they do in crime novels. They just talk about it."

"I'm game. Saves gas."

We got back to the house and sat across from each other at the kitchen table. Amelia brewed a cup of tea for herself, while I got a caffeine-free Coke.

I said, "Greg is scared that someone is going through his files at work. We solved the part about someone being in his office. That was the daughter and her boyfriend. So we're left with the files. Now, who would be interested in Greg's clients?"

"There's always the chance that some client doesn't think Greg paid out enough on a claim, or maybe thinks Greg is cheating his clients." Amelia took a sip of her tea.

"But why go through the files? Why not just bring a complaint to the national insurance agents' board, or whatever?"

"Okay. Then there's . . . the only other answer is another insurance agent. Someone who wonders why Greg has such phenomenal luck in what he insures. Someone who doesn't believe it's chance or those cheesy synthetic rabbits' feet."

It was so simple when you thought about it, when you cleared away the mental debris. I was sure the culprit had to be someone in the same business.

I was pretty sure I knew the other three insurance agents in Bon Temps, but I checked the phone book to be sure.

"I suggest we go from agent to agent, starting with the local ones," Amelia said. "I'm relatively new in town, so I can tell them I want to take out some more insurance."

"I'll come with you, and I'll scan them."

"During the conversation, I'll bring up the Aubert Agency, so they'll be thinking about the right thing." Amelia had asked enough questions to understand how my telepathy worked.

I nodded. "First thing tomorrow morning."

We went to sleep that night with a pleasant tingle of anticipation. A plan was a beautiful thing. Stackhouse and Broadway swing into action.

The next day didn't start exactly like we'd planned. For one thing, the weather had decided to be fall. It was cool. It was pouring rain. I put my shorts and tank tops away sadly, knowing I probably wouldn't wear them again for several months.

The first agent, Diane Porchia, was guarded by a meek clerk. Alma Dean crumpled like a fender when we insisted on seeing the actual agent. Amelia, with her bright smile and gorgeous teeth, simply beamed at Ms. Dean until she called Diane out of her office. The middle-aged agent, a stocky woman in a green pantsuit, came out to shake our hands. I said, "I've been taking my friend Amelia around to all the agents in town, starting with Greg Aubert." I was listening as hard as I could to the result, and all I got was professional pride . . . and a hint of desperation. Diane Porchia was scared by the number of claims she had processed lately. It was abnormally high. All she was thinking of was selling. Amelia gave me a little hand wave. Diane Porchia was not a magical null.

"Greg Aubert thought he'd had someone break into his office at night," Amelia said.

"Us, too," Diane said, seeming genuinely astonished. "But nothing was taken." She rallied and got back to her purpose. "Our rates are very competitive with anything Greg can offer you. Take a look at the coverage we provide, and I think you'll agree."

Shortly after that, our heads filled with figures, we were on our way to Bailey Smith. Bailey was a high school classmate of my brother Jason's, and we had to spend a little longer there playing "What's he/she doing now?" But the result was the same. Bailey's only concern was getting Amelia's business, and maybe getting her to go out for a drink with him if he could think of a place to take her that his wife wouldn't hear about.

He had had a break-in at his office, too. In his case, the window had been shattered. But nothing had been taken. And I heard directly from his brain that business was down. Way down.

At John Robert Briscoe's we had a different problem. He didn't want to see us. His clerk, Sally Lundy, was like an angel with a flaming sword guarding the entrance to his private office. We got our chance when a client came in, a little withered woman who'd had a collision the month before. She said, "I don't know how this could be, but the minute I signed with John Robert, I had an accident. Then a month goes by, and I have another one."

"Come on back, Mrs. Hanson." Sally gave us a mistrustful look as she took the little woman to the inner sanctum. The minute they were gone, Amelia went through the stack of paperwork in the in-box, to my surprise and dismay.

Sally came back to her desk, and Amelia and I took our departure. I said, "We'll come back later. We've got another appointment right now."

"They were all claims," Amelia said, when we were out of the door. "Every one of them." She pushed back the hood on her slicker since the rain had finally stopped.

"There's something wrong with that. John Robert has been hit even harder than Diane or Bailey."

We stared at each other. Finally, I said what we were both thinking. "Did Greg upset some balance by claiming more than his fair share of good luck?"

"I never heard of such a thing," Amelia said. But we both believed that Greg had unwittingly tipped over a cosmic applecart.

"There weren't any nulls at any of the other agencies," Amelia said. "It's got to be John Robert or his clerk. I didn't get to check either of them."

"He'll be going to lunch any minute," I said, glancing down at my watch. "Probably Sally will be, too. I'll go to the back where they park and stall them. Do you just have to be close?"

"If I have one of my spells, it'll be

244

better," she said. She darted over to the car and unlocked it, pulling out her purse. I hurried around to the back of the building, just a block off the main street but surrounded by crepe myrtles.

I managed to catch John Robert as he left his office to go to lunch. His car was dirty. His clothes were disheveled. He slumped. I knew him by sight, but we'd never had a conversation.

"Mr. Briscoe," I said, and his head swung up. He seemed confused. Then his face cleared, and he tried to smile.

"Sookie Stackhouse, right? Girl, it's been an age since I saw you."

"I guess you don't come in Merlotte's much."

"No, I pretty much go home to the

wife and kids in the evening," he said. "They've got a lot of activities."

"Do you ever go over to Greg Aubert's office?" I asked, trying to sound gentle.

He stared at me for a long moment. "No, why would I do that?"

And I could tell, hear from his head directly, that he absolutely didn't know what I was talking about. But there came Sally Lundy, steam practically coming out of her ears at the sight of me talking to her boss when she'd done her best to shield him.

"Sally," John Robert said, relieved to see his right-hand woman, "this young woman wants to know if I've been to Greg's office lately."

"I'll just bet she does," Sally said, and even John Robert blinked at the venom in her voice.

And I got it then, the name I'd been waiting for.

"It's you," I said. "You're the one, Ms. Lundy. What are you doing that for?" If I hadn't known I had backup, I would've been scared. Speaking of backup . . .

"What am I doing it for?" she screeched. "You have the gall, the nerve, the . . . the *balls* to ask me that?"

John Robert couldn't have looked more horrified if she'd sprouted horns.

"Sally," he said, very anxiously. "Sally, maybe you need to sit down."

"You can't see it!" she shrieked. "You can't see it. That Greg Aubert, he's dealing with the devil! Diane and Bailey are in the same boat we are, and it's sinking! Do you know how many claims he had to handle last week? Three! Do you know how many new policies he wrote? Thirty!"

John Robert literally staggered when he heard the numbers. He recovered enough to say, "Sally, we can't make wild accusations against Greg. He's a fine man. He'd never . . ."

But Greg had, however blindly.

Sally decided it would be a good time to kick me in the shins, and I was really glad I was wearing jeans instead of shorts that day. *Okay, anytime now, Amelia,* I thought. John Robert was windmilling his arms and yelling at Sally — though not moving to restrain her, I noticed — and Sally was yelling back at the top of her lungs and venting her feelings about Greg Aubert and that bitch Marge who worked for him. She had a lot to say about Marge. No love lost there.

By that time I was holding Sally off at arm's length, and I was sure my legs would be black-and-blue the next day.

Finally, *finally,* Amelia appeared, breathless and disarranged. "Sorry," she panted, "you're not going to believe this, but my foot got stuck between the car seat and the doorsill, then I fell, and my keys went under the car . . . anyway, *Congelo!*"

Sally's foot stopped in midswing, so she was balancing on one skinny leg. John Robert had both hands in the air in a gesture of despair. I touched his arm, and he felt as hard as the frozen vampire had the other night. At least he wasn't holding me.

"Now what?" I asked.

"I thought you knew!" she said. "We've got to get them off thinking about Greg and his luck!"

"The problem is, I think Greg's used up all the luck going around," I said. "Look at the problems you had just getting out of the car here."

She looked intensely thoughtful. "Yeah, we have to have a chat with Greg," she said. "But first, we've got to get out of this situation." Holding out her right hand toward the two frozen people, she said, "Ah — *amicus cum Greg Aubert.*"

They didn't look any more amiable, but maybe the change was taking place in their hearts. *"Regelo,"* Amelia said, and Sally's foot came down to the ground hard. The older woman lurched a bit, and I caught her. "Watch out, Miss Sally," I said, hoping she wouldn't kick me again. "You were a little off balance there."

She looked at me in surprise. "What are you doing back here?"

Good question. "Amelia and I were just cutting through the parking lot on our way to McDonald's," I said, gesturing toward the golden arches that stuck up one street over. "We didn't realize that you had so many high bushes around the back, here. We'll just return to the front parking lot and get our car and drive around."

"That would be better," John Robert said. "That way we wouldn't have to worry about something happening to your car while it was parked in our parking lot." He looked gloomy again. "Something's sure to hit it, or fall on top of it. Maybe I'll just call that nice Greg Aubert and ask him if he's got any ideas about breaking my streak of bad luck."

"You do that," I said. "Greg would be glad to talk to you. He'll give you lots of his lucky rabbits' feet, I bet."

"Yep, that Greg sure is nice," Sally Lundy agreed. She turned to back into the office, a little dazed but none the worse for wear.

Amelia and I went over to the Pelican State office. We were both feeling pretty thoughtful about the whole thing.

Greg was in, and we plopped down on the client side of his desk.

"Greg, you've got to stop using the spells so much," I said, and I explained why.

Greg looked frightened and angry. "But I'm the best agent in Louisiana. I have an incredible record."

"I can't make you change anything, but you're sucking up all the luck in Renard Parish," I said. "You gotta let loose of some of it for the other guys. Diane and Bailey are hurting so much they're thinking about changing professions. John Robert Briscoe is almost suicidal." To do Greg credit, once we explained the situation, he was horrified.

"I'll modify my spells," he said. "I'll accept some of the bad luck. I just can't believe I was using up everyone else's share." He still didn't look happy, but he was resigned. "And the people in the office at night?" Greg asked meekly.

"Don't worry about it," I said. "Taken care of." At least, I hoped so. Just because Bill had taken the young vampire to Shreveport to see Eric didn't mean that he wouldn't come back again. But maybe the couple would find somewhere else to conduct their mutual exploration.

"Thank you," Greg said, shaking our hands. In fact, Greg cut us a check, which was also nice, though we assured him it wasn't necessary. Amelia looked proud and happy. I felt pretty cheerful myself. We'd cleaned up a couple of the world's problems, and things were better because of us.

"We were fine investigators," I said, as we drove home.

"Of course," said Amelia. "We weren't just good. We were lucky."

■ ■ ■ ■

GIFT WRAP

■ ■ ■ ■

It was Christmas Eve. I was all by myself.

Does that sound sad and pathetic enough to make you say, "Poor Sookie Stackhouse!"? You don't need to. I was feeling plenty sorry for myself, and the more I thought about my solitude at this time of the year, the more my eyes welled and my chin quivered.

Most people hang with their family and friends at the holiday season. I actually do have a brother, but we aren't speaking. I'd recently discovered I have a living great-grandfather, though I didn't believe he would even realize it was Christmas. (Not because he's senile — far from it — but because he's not a Christian.) Those two are it for me, as far as close family goes.

I actually do have friends, too, but they all seemed to have their own plans this year. Amelia Broadway, the witch who lives on the top floor of my house, had driven down to New Orleans to spend the holiday with her father. My friend and employer, Sam Merlotte, had gone home to Texas to see his mom, stepfather, and siblings. My childhood friends Tara and JB would be spending Christmas Eve with JB's family; plus, it was their first Christmas as a married couple. Who could horn in on that? I had other friends . . . friends close enough that if I'd made puppy-dog eyes when they were talking about their holiday plans, they would have included me on their guest list in a heartbeat. In a fit of perversity, I hadn't wanted to be pitied for being alone. I guess I wanted to manage that all by myself.

Sam had gotten a substitute bartender, but Merlotte's Bar closes at two o'clock in the afternoon on Christmas Eve and remains closed until two o'clock the day after Christmas, so I didn't even have work to break up a lovely uninterrupted stretch of misery.

My laundry was done. The house was clean. The week before, I'd put up my grandmother's Christmas decorations, which I'd inherited along with the house. Opening the boxes of ornaments made me miss my grandmother with a sharp ache. She'd been gone almost two years, and I still wished I could talk to her. Not only had Gran been a lot of fun, she'd been really shrewd and she'd given good advice — if she decided you really needed some. She'd raised me from the age of seven, and she'd been the most important figure in my life.

She'd been so pleased when I'd started dating the vampire Bill Compton. That was how desperate Gran had been for me to get a beau; even Vampire Bill was welcome. When you're telepathic like I am, it's hard to date a regular guy; I'm sure you can see why. Humans think all kinds of things they don't want their nearest and dearest to know about, much less a woman they're taking out to dinner and a movie. In sharp contrast, vampires' brains are lovely silent blanks to me, and werewolf brains are nearly as good as vampires', though I get a big waft of emotions and the odd snatch of thought from my occasionally furred acquaintances.

Naturally, after I'd thought about Gran welcoming Bill, I began wondering what Bill was doing. Then I rolled my eyes at my own idiocy. It was mid-afternoon, daytime. Bill was sleeping somewhere in his house, which lay in the woods to the south of my place, across the cemetery. I'd broken up with Bill, but I was sure he'd be over like a shot if I called him — once darkness fell, of course.

Damned if I would call him. Or anyone else.

But I caught myself staring longingly at the telephone every time I passed by. I needed to get out of the house or I'd be phoning someone, anyone.

I needed a mission. A project. A task. A diversion.

I remembered having awakened for about thirty seconds in the wee hours of the morning. Since I'd worked the late shift at Merlotte's, I'd only just sunk into a deep sleep. I'd stayed awake only long enough to wonder what had jarred me out of that sleep. I'd heard something out in the woods, I thought. The sound hadn't been repeated, and I'd dropped back into slumber like a stone into water.

Now I peered out the kitchen window at the woods. Not too surprisingly, there was nothing unusual about the view. "The woods are snowy, dark, and deep," I said, trying to recall the Frost poem we'd all had to memorize in high school. Or was it "lovely, dark, and deep"?

Of course, my woods weren't lovely *or* snowy — they never are in Louisiana at Christmas, even northern Louisiana. But it was cold (here, that meant the temperature was about thirty-eight degrees Fahrenheit). And the woods were definitely dark and deep — and damp. So I put on my lace-up work boots that I'd bought years before when my brother, Jason, and I had gone hunting together, and I shrugged into my heaviest "I don't care what happens to it" coat, really more of a puffy quilted jacket. It was pale pink. Since a heavy coat takes a long time to wear out down here, the coat was several years old, too; I'm twenty-seven, definitely past the pale pink stage. I bundled all my hair up under a knit cap, and I pulled on the gloves I'd found stuffed into one pocket. I hadn't worn this coat for a long, long time, and I was surprised to find a couple of dollars and some ticket stubs in the pockets, plus a receipt for a little Christmas gift I'd given Alcide Herveaux, a werewolf I'd dated briefly.

Pockets are like little time capsules. Since I'd bought Alcide the sudoku book, his father had died in a struggle for the job of packmaster, and after a series of violent events, Alcide himself ascended to the leadership. I wondered how pack affairs were going in

Shreveport. I hadn't talked to any of the Weres in two months. In fact, I'd lost track of when the last full moon had been. Last night?

Now I'd thought about Bill *and* Alcide. Unless I took action, I'd begin brooding over my most recent lost boyfriend, Quinn. It was time to get on the move.

My family has lived in this humble house for over a hundred and fifty years. My much-adapted home lies in a clearing in the middle of some woods off Hummingbird Road, outside of the small town of Bon Temps, in Renard Parish. The trees are deeper and denser to the east at the rear of the house, since they haven't been logged in a good fifty years. They're thinner on the south side, where the cemetery lies. The land is gently rolling, and far back on the property there's a little stream, but I hadn't walked all the way back to the stream in ages. My life had been very busy, what with hustling drinks at the bar, telepathing (is that a verb?) for the vampires, unwillingly participating in vampire and Were power struggles, and other magical and mundane stuff like that.

It felt good to be out in the woods, though the air was raw and damp, and it felt good to be using my muscles.

I made my way through the brush for at least thirty minutes, alert for any indication of what had caused the ruckus the night before. There are lots of animals indigenous to northern Louisiana, but most of them are quiet and shy: possums, raccoons, deer. Then there are the slightly less quiet but still shy mammals, like coyotes and foxes. We have a few more formidable creatures. In the bar, I hear hunters' stories all the time. A couple of the more enthusiastic sportsmen had glimpsed a black bear on a private hunting preserve about two miles from my house. And Terry Bellefleur had sworn to me he'd seen a panther less than two years ago. Most of the avid hunters had spotted feral hogs, razorbacks.

Of course, I wasn't expecting to encounter anything like that. I had popped my cell phone into my pocket, just in case, though I wasn't sure I could get a signal out in the woods.

By the time I'd worked my way through the thick woods to the stream, I was warm inside the puffy coat. I was ready to crouch down for a minute or two to examine the soft ground by the water. The stream, never big to begin with, was level with its banks after the recent rainfall. Though I'm not Nature Girl, I could tell that deer had been here; raccoons, too; and maybe a dog. Or two. Or three. *That's not good,* I thought with a hint of unease. A pack of dogs always had the potential to become dangerous. I wasn't anywhere near savvy enough to tell how old the tracks were, but I would have expected them to look drier if they'd been made over a day ago.

There was a sound from the bushes to my left. I froze, scared to raise my face and turn in toward the right direction. I slipped my cell phone out of my pocket, looked at the bars. OUTSIDE OF AREA, read the legend on the little screen. *Crap,* I thought. That hardly began to cover it.

The sound was repeated. I decided it was a moan. Whether it had issued from man or beast, I didn't know. I bit my lip, hard, and then I made myself stand up, very slowly and carefully. Nothing happened. No more sounds. I got a grip on myself and edged cautiously to my left. I pushed aside a big stand of laurel.

There was a man lying on the ground, in the cold wet mud. He was naked as a jaybird, but patterned in dried blood.

I approached him cautiously, because even naked, bleeding, muddy men could be mighty dangerous; maybe *especially* dangerous.

"Ah," I said. As an opening statement, that left a lot to be desired. "Ah, do you need help?" Okay, that ranked right up there with "How do you feel?" as a stupid opening statement.

His eyes opened — tawny eyes, wild and round like an owl's. "Get away," he said urgently. "They may be coming back."

"Then we'd better hurry," I said. I had no intention of leaving an injured man in the path of whatever had injured him in the first place. "How bad are you hurt?"

"No, *run,*" he said. "It's not long until dark." Painfully, he stretched out a hand to grip my ankle. He definitely wanted me to pay attention.

It was really hard to listen to his

words since there was a lot of bareness that kept my eyes busy. I resolutely focused my gaze above his chest. Which was covered, not too thickly, with dark brown hair. Across a broad expanse. Not that I was looking!

"Come on," I said, kneeling beside the stranger. A mélange of prints indented the mud, indicating a lot of activity right around him. "How long have you been here?"

"A few hours," he said, gasping as he tried to prop himself up on one elbow.

"In this cold?" Geez Louise. No wonder his skin was bluish. "We got to get you indoors," I said. "Now." I looked from the blood on his left shoulder to the rest of him, trying to spot other injuries.

That was a mistake. The rest of him — though visibly muddy, bloody, and cold — was really, really . . .

What was wrong with me? Here I was, looking at a complete (naked and handsome) stranger with lust, while he was scared and wounded. "Here," I said, trying to sound resolute and determined and neutered. "Put your good arm around my neck, and we'll get you to your knees. Then you can get up, and we can start moving."

There were bruises all over him, but not another injury that had broken the skin, I thought. He protested several more times, but the sky was getting darker as the night drew in, and I cut him off sharply. "Get a move on," I advised him. "We don't want to be out here any longer than we have to be. It's going to take the better part of an hour to get you to the house."

The man fell silent. He finally nodded. With a lot of work, we got him to his feet. I winced when I saw how scratched and filthy they were.

"Here we go," I said encouragingly. He took a step, did a little wincing of his own. "What's your name?" I said, trying to distract him from the pain of walking.

"Preston," he said. "Preston Pardloe."

"Where you from, Preston?" We were moving a little faster now, which was good. The woods were getting darker and darker.

"I'm from Baton Rouge," he said. He sounded a little surprised.

"And how'd you come to be in my

woods?"

"Well . . ."

I realized what his problem was. "Are you a Were, Preston?" I asked. I felt his body relax against my own. I'd known it already from his brain pattern, but I didn't want to scare him by telling him about my little disability. Preston had a — how can I describe it? — a smoother, thicker pattern than other Weres I'd encountered, but each mind has its own texture.

"Yes," he said. "You know, then."

"Yeah," I said. "I know." I knew way more than I'd ever wanted to. Vampires had come out in the open with the advent of the Japanese-marketed synthetic blood that could sustain them, but other creatures of the night and shadows hadn't yet taken the same giant step.

"What pack?" I asked, as we stumbled over a fallen branch and recovered. He was leaning on me heavily. I feared we'd actually tumble to the ground. We needed to pick up the pace. He did seem to be moving more easily now that his muscles had warmed up a little.

"The Deer Killer pack, from south of Baton Rouge."

"What are you doing up here in my woods?" I asked again.

"This land is yours? I'm sorry we trespassed," he said. His breath caught as I helped him around a devil's walking stick. One of the thorns caught in my pink coat, and I pulled it out with difficulty.

"That's the least of my worries," I said. "Who attacked you?"

"The Sharp Claw pack from Monroe."

I didn't know any Monroe Weres.

"Why were you here?" I asked, thinking sooner or later he'd have to answer me if I kept asking.

"We were supposed to meet on neutral ground," he said, his face tense with pain. "A werepanther from out in the country somewhere offered the land to us as a midway point, a neutral zone. Our packs have been . . . feuding. He said this would be a good place to resolve our differences."

My brother had offered my land as a Were parley ground? The stranger and I struggled along in silence while I tried to think that through. My brother, Jason, was indeed a werepanther, though he'd become one by being bitten; his estranged wife was a born werepanther, a genetic panther. What was Jason thinking, sending such a dangerous gathering my way? Not of my welfare, that's for sure.

Granted, we weren't on good terms, but it was painful to think he'd actually want to do me harm. Any more than he'd already done me, that is.

A hiss of pain brought my attention back to my companion. Trying to help him more efficiently, I put my arm around his waist, and he draped his arm across my shoulder. We were able to make better time that way, to my relief. Five minutes later, I saw the light I'd left on above the back porch.

"Thank God," I said. We began moving faster, and we reached the house just as dark fell. For a second, my companion arched and tensed, but he didn't change. That was a relief.

Getting up the steps turned into an ordeal, but finally I got Preston into the house and seated at the kitchen table. I looked him over anxiously. This wasn't the first time I'd brought a bleeding and naked man into my kitchen, oddly enough. I'd found a vampire named Eric under similar circumstances. Was that not incredibly weird, even for my life? Of course, I didn't have time to mull that over, because this man needed some attention.

I tried to look at the shoulder wound in the improved light of the kitchen, but he was so grimy it was hard to examine in detail. "Do you think you could stand to take a shower?" I asked, hoping I didn't sound like I thought he smelled or anything. Actually, he did smell a little unusual, but his scent wasn't unpleasant.

"I think I can stay upright that long," he said briefly.

"Okay, stay put for a second," I said. I brought the old afghan from the back of the living room couch and arranged it around him carefully. Now it was easier to concentrate.

I hurried to the hall bathroom to turn on the shower controls, added long after the claw-footed bathtub had been installed. I leaned over to turn on the water, waited until it was hot, and got out two fresh towels. Amelia had left shampoo and crème rinse in the rack hanging from the showerhead, and there was plenty of soap. I put my hand under the water. Nice and hot.

"Okay!" I called. "I'm coming to get you!"

My unexpected visitor was looking startled when I got back to the kitchen. "For what?" he asked, and I wondered if he'd hit his head in the woods.

"For the shower. Hear the water running?" I said, trying to sound matter-of-fact. "I can't see the extent of your wounds until I get you clean."

We were up and moving again, and I thought he was walking better, as if the warmth of the house and the smoothness of the floor helped his muscles relax. He'd just left the afghan on the chair. No problem with nudity, like most Weres, I noticed. Okay, that was good, right? His thoughts were opaque to me, as Were thoughts sometimes were, but I caught flashes of anxiety.

Suddenly he leaned against me much more heavily, and I staggered into the wall. "Sorry," he said, gasping. "Just had a twinge in my leg."

"No problem," I said. "It's probably your muscles stretching." We made it into the small bathroom, which was very old-fashioned. My own bathroom off my bedroom was more modern, but this was less personal.

But Preston didn't seem to note the black-and-white-checkered tile. With unmistakable eagerness, he was eyeing the hot water spraying down into the tub.

"Ah, do you need me to leave you alone for a second before I help you into the shower?" I asked, indicating the toilet with a tip of my head.

He looked at me blankly. "Oh," he said, finally understanding. "No, that's all right." So we made it to the side of the tub, which was a high one. With a lot of awkward maneuvering, Preston swung a leg over the side, and I shoved, and he was able to raise the second leg enough to climb completely in. After making sure he could stand by himself, I began to pull the shower curtain closed.

"Lady," he said, and I stopped. He was under the stream of hot water, his hair plastered to his head, water beating on his chest and running down to drip off his . . . Okay, he'd gotten warmer everywhere.

"Yes?" I was trying not to sound like I was choking.

"What's your name?"

"Oh! Excuse me." I swallowed hard. "My name is Sookie. Sookie Stackhouse." I swallowed again. "There's the soap; there's the shampoo. I'm going to leave the bathroom door open, okay? You just call me when you're through, and I'll help you out of the tub."

"Thanks," he said. "I'll yell if I need you."

I pulled the shower curtain, not without regret. After checking that the clean towels were where Preston could easily reach them, I returned to the kitchen. I wondered if he would like coffee or hot chocolate or tea? Or maybe alcohol? I had some bourbon, and there were a couple of beers in the refrigerator. I'd ask him. Soup, he'd need some soup. I didn't have any homemade, but I had Campbell's Chicken Tortilla. I put the soup into a pan on the stove, got coffee ready to go, and boiled some water in case he opted for the chocolate or tea. I was practically vibrating with purpose.

When Preston emerged from the bathroom, his bottom half was wrapped in a large blue bath towel of Amelia's. Believe me, it had never looked so good. Preston had draped a towel around his neck to catch the drips from his hair, and it covered his shoulder wound. He winced a little as he walked, and I knew his feet must be sore. I'd gotten some men's socks by mistake on my last trip to Wal-Mart, so I got them from my drawer and handed them to Preston, who'd resumed his seat at the table. He looked at them very carefully, to my puzzlement.

"You need to put on some socks," I said, wondering if he paused because he thought he was wearing some other man's garments. "They're mine," I said reassuringly. "Your feet must be tender."

"Yes," said Preston, and rather slowly, he bent to put them on.

"You need help?" I was pouring the soup in a bowl.

"No, thank you," he said, his face hidden by his thick dark hair as he bent to the task. "What smells so good?"

"I heated some soup for you," I said. "You want coffee or tea or . . ."

"Tea, please," he said.

I never drank tea myself, but Amelia had some. I looked through her selection, hoping none of these blends would turn him into a frog or anything. Amelia's magic had had unexpected results in the past. Surely anything marked LIPTON was okay? I dunked the tea bag into the scalding water and hoped for the best.

Preston ate the soup carefully. Maybe I'd gotten it too hot. He spooned it into his mouth like he'd never had soup before. Maybe his mama had always served homemade. I felt a little embarrassed. I was staring at him, because I sure didn't have anything better to look at. He looked up and met my eyes.

Whoa. Things were moving too fast here. "So, how'd you get hurt?" I asked. "Was there a skirmish? How come your pack left you?"

"There was a fight," he said. "Negotiations didn't work." He looked a little doubtful and distressed. "Somehow, in the dark, they left me."

"Do you think they're coming back to get you?"

He finished his soup, and I put his tea down by his hand. "Either my own pack or the Monroe one," he said grimly.

That didn't sound good. "Okay, you better let me see your wounds now," I said. The sooner I knew his fitness level, the sooner I could decide what to do. Preston removed the towel from around his neck, and I bent to look at the wound. It was almost healed.

"When were you hurt?" I asked.

"Toward dawn." His huge tawny eyes met mine. "I lay there for hours."

"But . . ." Suddenly I wondered if

I'd been entirely intelligent, bringing a stranger into my home. I knew it wasn't wise to let Preston know I had doubts about his story. The wound had looked jagged and ugly when I'd found him in the woods. Yet now that he came into the house, it healed in a matter of minutes? What was up? Weres healed fast, but not instantly.

"What's wrong, Sookie?" he asked. It was pretty hard to think about anything else when his long wet hair was trailing across his chest and the blue towel was riding pretty low.

"Are you really a Were?" I blurted, and backed up a couple of steps. His brain waves dipped into the classic Were rhythm, the jagged, dark cadence I found familiar.

Preston Pardloe looked absolutely horrified. "What else would I be?" he said, extending an arm. Obligingly, fur rippled down from his shoulder and his fingers clawed. It was the most effortless change I'd ever seen, and there was very little of the noise I associated with the transformation, which I'd witnessed several times.

"You must be some kind of super werewolf," I said.

"My family is gifted," he said proudly.

He stood, and his towel slipped off.

"No kidding," I said in a strangled voice. I could feel my cheeks turning red.

There was a howl outside. There's no eerier sound, especially on a dark, cold night; and when that eerie sound comes from the line where your yard meets the woods, well, that'll make the hairs on your arm stand up. I glanced at Preston's wolfy arm to see if the howl had had the same effect on him, and saw that his arm had reverted to human shape.

"They've returned to find me," he said.

"Your pack?" I said, hoping that his kin had returned to retrieve him.

"No." His face was bleak. "The Sharp Claws."

"Call your people. Get them here."

"They left me for a reason." He looked humiliated. "I didn't want to talk about it. But you've been so kind."

I was not liking this more and more. "And that reason would be?"

"I was payment for an offense."

"Explain in twenty words or less."

He stared down at the floor, and I realized he was counting in his head.

This guy was one of a kind. "Pack-leader's sister wanted me, I didn't want her, she said I'd insulted her, my torture was the price."

"Why would your packleader agree to any such thing?"

"Am I still supposed to number my words?"

I shook my head. He'd sounded dead serious. Maybe he just had a really deep sense of humor.

"I'm not my packleader's favorite person, and he was willing to believe I was guilty. He himself wants the sister of the Sharp Claw packmaster, and it would be a good match from the point of view of our packs. So, I was hung out to dry."

I could sure believe that the pack-master's sister had lusted after him. The rest of the story was not outrageous, if you've had many dealings with the Weres. Sure, they're all human and reasonable on the outside, but when they're in their Were mode, they're different.

"So, they're here to get you and keep on beating you up?"

He nodded somberly. I didn't have the heart to tell him to rewind the towel. I took a deep breath, looked away, and decided I'd better go get the shotgun.

Howls were echoing, one after another, through the night by the time I fetched the shotgun from the closet in the living room. The Sharp Claws had tracked Preston to my house, clearly. There was no way I could hide him and say that he'd gone. Or was there? If they didn't come in . . .

"You need to get in the vampire

hole," I said. Preston turned from staring at the back door, his eyes widening as he took in the shotgun. "It's in the guest bedroom." The vampire hole dated from when Bill Compton had been my boyfriend, and we'd thought it was prudent to have a light-tight place at my house in case he got caught by day.

When the big Were didn't move, I grabbed his arm and hustled him down the hall, showed him the trick bottom of the bedroom closet. Preston started to protest — all Weres would rather fight than flee — but I shoved him in, lowered the "floor," and threw the shoes and junk back in there to make the closet look realistic.

There was a loud knock at the front door. I checked the shotgun to make sure it was loaded and ready to fire, and then I went into the living room. My heart was pounding about a hundred miles a minute.

Werewolves tend to take blue-collar jobs in their human lives, though some of them parlay those jobs into business empires. I looked through my peephole to see that the werewolf at my front door must be a semipro wrestler. He was huge. His hair hung in tight gelled waves to his shoulders, and he had a trimmed beard and mustache, too. He was wearing a leather vest and leather pants and motorcycle boots. He actually had leather strips tied around his upper arms, and leather braces on his wrists. He looked like someone from a fetish magazine.

"What do you want?" I called through the door.

"Let me come in," he said, in a surprisingly high voice.

Little pig, little pig, let me come in!

"Why would I do that?" *Not by the hair of my chinny-chin-chin.*

"Because we can break in if we have to. We got no quarrel with you. We know this is your land, and your brother told us you know all about us. But we're tracking a guy, and we gotta know if he's in there."

"There was a guy here, he came up to my back door," I called. "But he made a phone call and someone came and picked him up."

"Not out here," the mountainous Were said.

"No, the back door." That was where Preston's scent would lead.

"Hmmmm." By pressing my ear to the door, I could hear the Were mutter, "Check it out," to a large dark form, which loped away. "I still gotta come in and check," my unwanted visitor said. "If he's in there, you might be in danger."

He should have said that first, to convince me he was trying to save me.

"Okay, but only you," I said. "And you know I'm a friend of the Shreveport pack, and if anything happens to me, you'll have to answer to them. Call Alcide Herveaux if you don't believe me."

"Oooo, I'm scared," said Man Mountain in an assumed falsetto. But as I swung open the front door and he got a look at the shotgun, I could see that he truly did look as if he was having second thoughts. Good.

I stood aside, keeping the Benelli

pointed in his direction to show I meant business. He strode through the house, his nose working all the time. His sense of smell wouldn't be nearly as accurate in his human form, and if he started to change, I intended to tell him I'd shoot if he did.

Man Mountain went upstairs, and I could hear him opening closets and looking under beds. He even stepped into the attic. I heard the creak its old door makes when it swings open.

Then he clomped downstairs in his big old boots. He was dissatisfied with his search, I could tell, because he was practically snorting. I kept the shotgun level.

Suddenly he threw back his head and roared. I flinched, and it was all I could do to hold my ground. My arms were exhausted.

He was glaring at me from his great height. "You're pulling something on us, woman. If I find out what it is, I'll be back."

"You've checked, and he's not here. Time to go. It's Christmas Eve, for goodness' sake. Go home and wrap some presents."

With a final look around the living room, out he went. I couldn't believe it. The bluff had worked. I lowered the gun and set it carefully back in the closet. My arms were trembling from holding it at the ready. I shut and locked the door behind him.

Preston was padding down the hall in the socks and nothing else, his face anxious.

"Stop!" I said, before he could step into the living room. The curtains were open. I walked around shutting all the curtains in the house, just to be on the safe side. I took the time to send out my special sort of search, and there were no live brains in the area around the house. I'd never been sure how far this ability could reach, but at least I knew the Sharp Claws were gone.

When I turned around after drawing the last drape, Preston was behind me, and then he had his arms around me, and then he was kissing me. I swam to the surface to say, "I don't really . . ."

"Pretend you found me gift-wrapped under the tree," he whispered. "Pretend you have mistletoe."

It was pretty easy to pretend both those things. Several times. Over hours.

When I woke up Christmas morning, I was as relaxed as a girl can be. It took me a while to figure out that Preston was gone; and while I felt a pang, I also felt just a bit of relief. I didn't know the guy, after all, and even after we'd been up close and personal, I had to wonder how a day alone with him would have gone. He'd left me a note in the kitchen.

"Sookie, you're incredible. You saved my life and gave me the best Christmas Eve I've ever had. I don't want to get you in any more trouble. I'll never forget how great you were in every way." He'd signed it.

I felt let down, but oddly enough I also felt happy. It was Christmas Day. I went in and plugged in the lights on the tree and sat on the old couch with my grandmother's afghan wrapped around me, which still smelled faintly of my visitor. I had a big mug of coffee and some home-made banana nut bread to have for breakfast. I had presents to unwrap. And about noon, the phone began to ring. Sam called, and Amelia; and even Jason called just to say "Merry Christmas, Sis." He hung up before I could charge him with loaning my land out to two packs of Weres. Considering the satisfying outcome, I decided to forgive and forget — at least that one transgression. I put my turkey breast in the oven, and fixed a sweet potato casserole, and opened a can of cranberry sauce, and made some cornbread dressing and some broccoli and cheese.

About thirty minutes before the somewhat simplified feast was ready, the doorbell rang. I was wearing a new pale blue pants and top outfit in velour, a gift from Amelia. I was feeling self-sufficient as hell.

I was astonished how happy I was to see my great-grandfather at the door. His name's Niall Brigant, and he's a fairy prince. Okay, long story, but that's what he is. I'd only met him a few weeks before, and I couldn't say we really knew each other well, but he was family. He's about six feet tall, he almost always wears a black suit with a white shirt and a black tie, and he has pale golden hair as fine as cornsilk; it's longer than my hair, and it seems to float around his head if there's the slightest breeze.

Oh, yeah, my great-grandfather is over a thousand years old. Or thereabouts. I guess it's hard to keep track after all those years.

Niall smiled at me. All the tiny wrinkles that fissured his fine skin moved when he smiled, and somehow that just added to his charm. He had a load of wrapped boxes, to add to my general level of amazement.

"Please come in, Great-grandfather," I said. "I'm so happy to see you! Can you have Christmas dinner with me?"

"Yes," he said. "That's why I've come. Though," he added, "I was not invited."

"Oh," I said, feeling ridiculously ill-mannered. "I just never thought you'd be interested in coming. I mean, after all, you're not . . ." I hesitated, not wanting to be tacky.

"Not Christian," he said gently. "No, dear one, but you love Christmas, and I thought I would share it with you."

"Yay," I said.

I'd actually wrapped a present for him, intending to give it to him when I next encountered him (for seeing Niall was not a regular event), so I was able to bask in complete happiness. He gave me an opal necklace, I gave him some new ties (that black one had to go) and a Shreveport Mudbugs pennant (local color).

When the food was ready, we ate dinner, and he thought it was all very good.

It was a great Christmas.

The creature Sookie Stackhouse knew as Preston was standing in the woods. He could see Sookie and her great-grandfather moving around in the living room.

"She really is lovely, and sweet as nectar," he said to his companion, the hulking Were who'd searched Sookie's house. "I only had to use a touch of magic to get the attraction started."

"How'd Niall get you to do it?" asked the Were. He really was a were-wolf, unlike Preston, who was a fairy with a gift for transforming himself.

"Oh, he helped me out of a jam once," Preston said. "Let's just say it involved an elf and a warlock, and leave it at that. Niall said he wanted to make this human's Christmas very happy, that she had no family and was deserving." He watched rather wistfully as Sookie's figure crossed the window. "Niall set up the whole story tailored to her needs. She's not speaking to her brother, so he was the one who 'loaned out' her woods. She loves to help people, so I was 'hurt'; she loves to protect people, so I was 'hunted.' She hadn't had sex in a long time, so I seduced her." Preston sighed. "I'd love to do it all over again. It was wonderful, if you like humans. But Niall said no further contact, and his word is law."

"Why do you think he did all this for her?"

"I've no idea. How'd he rope you and Curt into this?"

"Oh, we work for one of his businesses as a courier. He knew we do a little community theater, that kind of thing." The Were looked unconvincingly modest. "So I got the part of Big Threatening Brute, and Curt was Other Brute."

"And a good job you did," Preston the fairy said bracingly. "Well, back to my own neck of the woods. See you later, Ralph."

" 'Bye now," Ralph said, and Preston popped out of sight.

"How the hell do they do that?" Ralph said, and stomped off through the woods to his waiting motorcycle and his buddy Curt. He had a pocketful of cash and a story he was charged to keep secret.

Inside the old house, Niall Brigant, fairy prince and loving great-grandfather, pricked his ears at the faint sound of Preston's and Ralph's departures. He knew it was audible to only his ears. He smiled down at his great-granddaughter. He didn't understand Christmas, but he understood that it was a time humans received and gave gifts, and drew together as families. As he looked at Sookie's happy face, he knew he had given her a unique yuletide memory.

"Merry Christmas, Sookie," he said, and kissed her on the cheek.

ABOUT THE AUTHOR

#1 *New York Times* bestselling author **Charlaine Harris** writes both fantasy and mystery. She lives in a small town in southern Arkansas with her family. Visit her website at www.charlaineharris.com.

We hope you have enjoyed this Large Print book. Other Thorndike, Wheeler, Kennebec, and Chivers Press Large Print books are available at your library or directly from the publishers.

For information about current and upcoming titles, please call or write, without obligation, to:

Publisher
Thorndike Press
295 Kennedy Memorial Drive
Waterville, ME 04901
Tel. (800) 223-1244

or visit our Web site at:

http://gale.cengage.com/thorndike

OR

Chivers Large Print
published by BBC Audiobooks Ltd
St James House, The Square
Lower Bristol Road
Bath BA2 3SB
England
Tel. +44(0) 800 136919
email: bbcaudiobooks@bbc.co.uk
www.bbcaudiobooks.co.uk

All our Large Print titles are designed for easy reading, and all our books are made to last.